THE HOUSE IN THE WOODS

YVETTE FIELDING

ANDERSEN PRESS

First published in 2021 by
Andersen Press Limited
20 Vauxhall Bridge Road, London SW1V 2SA
Vijverlaan 48, 3062 HL Rotterdam, Nederland
www.andersenpress.co.uk

4 6 8 10 9 7 5 3

All rights reserved. No part of this publication may be reproduced,
stored in a retrieval system or transmitted in any form, or by any
means, electronic, mechanical, photocopying, recording or
otherwise, without the written permission of the publisher.

The rights of Yvette Fielding to be identified as the author
of this work has been asserted by her in accordance with
the Copyright, Designs and Patents Act, 1988.

Text copyright © Yvette Fielding, 2021

British Library Cataloguing in Publication Data available.

ISBN 978 1 83913 114 1

Printed and bound in Great Britain by
Clays Ltd, Elcograf S.p.A.

CHAPTER 1

Halloween

The graveyard was still and deathly quiet. Only the hoot of a solitary owl could be heard in the distance. The moon was full, its light casting a milky glow over the ancient gravestones and magnificent mausoleums.

It came from below, a grey insipid wisp that grew in stature with every second, until finally its form settled into the shape of a tall man wearing a black cloak and top hat. The spectre floated off the ground, as if walking on air. His face was dark and menacing, eyes red with fury. From his open mouth thousands of insects took flight. He was looking for something: his next victim.

In life, this ghostly being had been a serial killer, a cruel murderer who preyed on the weak and innocent. Now the ghostly figure roamed the graveyard, searching for someone, anyone, to kill. But that wasn't possible. Unbeknown to him, he was dead; his destiny, his torture, was to roam this place for eternity.

He glided between the headstones looking all about him.

Sniffing the air, he seemed to have caught a scent. *What was it? Male? No . . . Female? Ah . . . both!*

Spying round the edge of a huge monolith, he saw them: three young people riding bicycles. The spirit grinned and smacked his lips. Tonight, they would be his.

As the three unsuspecting cyclists came closer, the demented ghost rushed towards them, arms out, eyes wide with rage. He heard their screams but could not seem to catch them. Enraged, he stopped, shaking with violent anger, watching them as they pedalled furiously away out of his reach. Maybe next time, he thought, as he made his long way back to his own pitiful unmarked grave.

Eve Proud, Tom Lake and Clovis Gayle's voices were shrill with nervous excitement. The three friends stood astride their bikes, looking wildly at each other, trying to catch their breath.

'What the hell was that?' screamed Eve, her eyes wild and cheeks flushed.

'I know, right! Was it real? It *seemed* real,' said Tom, looking behind him to check they were safe.

'Let me get this straight in my head. Did you just see what I saw? A tall man wearing a top hat?' said Eve, running her hands through her short blonde hair.

'Yes, I definitely saw him! And before you ask, Clovis, it *wasn't* a guy in a fancy-dress costume. It was a ghost! I *know* it was.' Tom glared at Clovis, who out of the three of them, was the most rational. Sometimes Clovis's insistence on logical explanations annoyed Tom, who was a total believer in the supernatural.

'I wasn't about to say that, Tom. I was actually going to agree with you. It could have been a memory being played out in front of us or . . .' Clovis continued in a whisper '. . . a man in a fancy-dress costume.'

'Oh, c'mon, Clovis, you saw it, it had red eyes, for God's sake!' Tom was becoming very impatient and more than a little frustrated with his friend.

'I can't deny it was very strange and it certainly scared me,' said Clovis, pushing his glasses back up the bridge of his nose.

'Well, whatever it was, it scared me to death,' said Eve. 'I don't think I've screamed that loud since we went on that horrendous ride at Thorpe Park. Come on, let's get out of here before it comes back. I don't think I'll sleep at all tonight.'

As the three friends pedalled out of the cemetery, Tom and Clovis were still arguing.

It was Friday the thirty-first of October, Halloween, and St Saviour's High School in East London was fully invested in the celebrations. Pumpkins lined the corridors, cardboard bats and spiders dangled from every classroom ceiling, and even a few of the teachers were wearing some very colourful costumes.

Eve, Tom and Clovis were in the last lesson of the day and quite enjoying it. Mr Mason, their history teacher, was reading from an old book about the Pagans and the origins of Halloween.

The teacher could tell by the look on some of his students' faces that the bell was about to ring. Eyes were glued to the clock on the wall. Any minute now, he thought.

Suddenly the loud clatter of the bell echoed through the classroom, and chairs scraped back, chatter and laughter erupting between friends.

'All right, guys, don't forget,' shouted Mr Mason above the din, 'I want five hundred words on Paganism and how it has impacted on our culture today. And I want it in my inbox first thing Monday morning.'

Everyone seemingly ignored him as they rampaged at high speed out of the classroom. However, Clovis hung back. He wanted to ask the teacher some more questions in private.

Clovis liked nothing more than research and spent most of his free time, when he wasn't with Eve and Tom, finding things out on the internet. He even designed apps and had his own blog, all under a secret name. The last thing Clovis wanted was his classmates to know what he really was: a nerd. He thought he seemed weird enough already; he was six feet tall, wore thick black-rimmed glasses, and had a name that was old-fashioned — although according to his mum, it was an honour to be named after his great-grandfather and he shouldn't be ashamed of it. To top it all off, he had a very soft voice. But Clovis had big dreams. One day he was going to become an inventor. He was going to invent things that would change the world.

His mum, Claudette, came from a respectable Jamaican family and wanted Clovis to do well at school. But she also wanted him to be happy and fit in. So, to please his mum, Clovis did just that. Or at least, he *tried* to fit in. Of course, Tom and Eve knew what a nerd he really was and they loved him for it. But he wanted to keep it a secret from everyone else.

After asking Mr Mason which websites he would recommend for further reading and discussing the similarity of Pagan festivals to Christian ones, Clovis left the classroom happy, and made his way out of the building to where Eve and Tom were waiting patiently for him.

'You ready, then?' asked Eve. Her black biker jacket was fastened up tightly and a scarf was wrapped snugly round her neck.

Tom was tapping his football from foot to foot and counting aloud: 'Thirty-four, thirty-five, thirty-six . . .'

Clovis barged his friend and kicked the ball away and the two teenagers wrestled each other.

'Guys!' shouted Eve, her impatience getting the better of her. 'C'mon, you both coming to mine later? Remember we're doing the *thing* tonight?' she added under her breath.

Tom and Clovis stopped messing about instantly.

'Yep,' said Clovis. 'Absolutely. I'm so intrigued.'

'Me too,' whispered Tom. 'But, I don't mind admitting, I'm a bit nervous about it now, especially after what we saw in the cemetery last night.'

'I've been thinking a lot about that,' said Clovis, 'and I think it was definitely someone dressed up, trying to scare us.'

'Yeah,' said Tom, 'I hate to admit it, but I think you might be right. It was just *too* good. The red eyes ruined it, really.'

'It was a great prank though,' said Eve. 'I totally believed it, nearly gave me a heart attack.'

'Hey, guys,' whispered Clovis. He leaned into his friends, not wanting anyone else to overhear what he was about to say. 'I know we want to scare ourselves tonight because it's Halloween, but do we *really* want to be messing with a Ouija board? I mean, you know I look for the logic in things but I did my research last night and there's enough evidence out there to suggest that a Ouija board really *does* act as some kind of portal to talk to dead people, and not always nice ones at that.'

'Are you kidding me?' hissed back Tom. 'You were the one who said it was all rubbish and that we should try it to prove that! It was *your* idea after watching that documentary on haunted houses. You said it would be fun and something for Halloween.'

'And,' pitched in Eve, '*quote*, "Seeing is believing." I've spent ages finding a board and the spooky location.'

'All right, I give in,' said Clovis, holding his hands up in surrender. 'We take the board with us tonight. But don't blame me if we get more than we bargained for.'

CHAPTER 2

An Inventor and a Bulldog

The three friends began the short walk back towards their homes. They all lived close to each other; Tom and Clovis since they were babies and Eve since she moved in with her uncle five years ago.

Tom lived with his mum and dad in a small house on the estate behind Eve and Clovis. Clovis lived with his mum and nineteen-year-old brother Jahmeel in one of the high-rise flats next to Eve's house.

Eve lived with her Uncle Rufus in a strange old twisted building that dated back to the fifteen-hundreds. With it being so old and having such historical importance to the community, the council could not demolish it, so when they constructed more properties, they just built around the old house instead.

The ancient building *did* look out of place, comical almost: a tall twisted black and white Tudor house that over the centuries had buckled and bent. The uneven windows looked out across the street towards huge high-rise flats that had seen better days. The little historical house that once would have been surrounded by farmland was now squashed between two more ugly high-rise flats. However, the quirky little home suited its residents perfectly.

Uncle Rufus was a little eccentric, a university professor by day and an inventor by night. Eve would often go to bed listening to the noises coming from his attic. Old jazz music softly filled the house, accompanied by the sounds of urgent hammering and sawing, mixed with some very loud rude words. The attic was his sanctuary, a place where he could research, invent new equipment and just be alone with his thoughts. Uncle Rufus loved the room at the top of the old house and didn't let anyone in except his British bulldog, Boris.

Of course, Clovis thought Uncle Rufus was a legend and had tried in vain to get access to the famous attic many times. What was he making up there? Eve would often report back to Clovis and Tom about some of the apparatus she saw her uncle carrying up the winding staircase. One day he brought home a trombone, a space hopper and a large copper bath, and Eve and her friends all sat at the top of the stairs listening to every sound they heard and trying to guess what he was making. They never did find out.

Now Eve clicked the front gate shut and walked up the stone steps. She put her key in the ancient lock and pushed open the heavy front door. As usual, Boris didn't move, but just lay there with his eyes half open, watching Eve take off her jacket. His little excuse for a tail wiggled as Eve stroked him.

'How's my lovely boy, then? I missed you today.'

Boris acknowledged Eve by licking her face and farting.

'Nice! Wow . . . that *stinks*.' Eve held her nose and walked up the long hallway, past photos of her mum, dad and her aunt Jess. Memories of happier times when they were all alive.

Five years earlier her parents and her aunt had been tragically killed in a train crash. Eve's mum and dad had died instantly, but Eve's aunt, Uncle Rufus's wife, had remained in a coma for three months until late one night she unexpectedly and sadly died too.

Uncle Rufus had always been a happy person and had been close to his sister, Eve's mum, so after the accident it was decided that Eve should go and live with him. He'd been good to her and helped her through those first few dreadful months when the pain of losing her parents was so raw and overwhelming. However, after Aunt Jess died, Uncle Rufus seemed to change. It was as if a light had gone out inside him. Although still loving and caring towards Eve, he seemed to have shut everyone else out of his life. Only Eve and his work seemed to matter and now he seemed to spend more and more time in his attic.

Eve set about making dinner for herself and her uncle. She knew it was unlikely that he'd have eaten anything all day. He just got so involved in his work, he forgot to eat. So, she scrambled eggs and buttered toast, then served it out onto two plates and put one of them on a tray with a napkin, cutlery and a glass of water. She took the tray up the creaking staircase to her uncle, round and round. Boris panted behind her. The poor dog hated those stairs, but Eve also knew he would go through anything to get to his master. Once at the top, she knocked on the attic door and called softly, 'Uncle, your dinner. I've brought it up for you.'

A clattering noise came from within the room followed by soft footsteps. Slowly the door creaked open and a pair of old-fashioned spectacles adorning a handsome, middle-aged face peered through the gap.

'Oh, how lovely, Eve! I'm famished. I would join you but . . . It's just I'm *so* close to finishing a project. I don't want to lose my momentum.' He put his hands out and took the tray from her.

'Good day?' he asked, opening the door a little wider with his foot so as to allow Boris in.

'Yep, it was OK I suppose . . . Er, Uncle, is it all right if I go out trick-or-treating with Tom and Clovis later?'

'Of course, of course, but make sure you're not back too late. You know how I worry.'

'Thanks, Unc, I promise.' Eve kissed her uncle's thin face and closed the door.

He was a kind man, Eve thought, and she loved him dearly, being the only family she had left. She wouldn't do anything to upset him and she *did* feel uncomfortable about lying to him, but she and her friends had been looking forward to this night for ages.

Clovis had been the one to introduce them to the world of the paranormal. Eve and Tom hadn't realised that ghost hunting was something you could actually do. Millions of people around the world went off in search of ghosts, Clovis had told them, and these people had all sorts of special equipment to capture paranormal activity when they spent the night in some very creepy places. Eve and Tom had watched the programmes and internet clips that Clovis had told them about. Instantly Eve had been transfixed, and along with her two friends had been fascinated by the idea of trying a ghost hunt themselves. Tonight was to be their first ghost hunt. After last night's excitement in the cemetery, she was keener than ever for their Halloween adventure to begin.

Taking two steps at a time, Eve rushed into the kitchen, bolted her dinner down and then ran back up the stairs into her bedroom where she began to pack her rucksack: three torches, a night-vision camera, and a Ouija board. She'd bought the board on the internet and the details and planning for tonight had mostly been her idea, even down to the spooky location. A few days ago, she had unexpectedly stumbled across a drawing of a house, a map and some notes left on the kitchen table. Normally her uncle never left his university work lying around, but on that particular morning he had left in a hurry and must have accidently forgotten the notes. They were for some sort of social history project, Eve figured, but as her uncle was a professor of science, not history, Eve wasn't sure why he had them. Anyway, according to the unfamiliar handwriting, the house was in Epping Forest and abandoned. It looked quite spooky from the picture and there were some footnotes about it being haunted. Eve had made a copy of the information and decided then and there that this would be the perfect location for their first ghost hunt. She hoped it would be a night to remember.

CHAPTER 3

Happy Families and Lies

Tom opened his front door and placed his football on top of the shoe rack. He took off his blazer and hung his backpack on the coat hook. His mum came into the cramped hallway drying her hands on a tea towel.

Angela Lake, or 'Ange' as her friends called her, was a frazzled and nervous woman, who spent all hours of the day running around after her husband Dan – or so it seemed to Tom.

'Quick, get in the kitchen, I've made you sausage, egg and chips for dinner. Eat it up sharpish, like, or your dad will 'ave 'em.'

Tom kissed his mum on the cheek and crept silently past the open doorway of the front room where his dad sat in an old threadbare armchair watching the horse racing on TV. He was eating a sausage sandwich and seemed unaware of the brown sauce that dripped down his large wobbly chin.

'Oi!' Dad shouted. 'Come 'ere, don't go creeping about. Did ya get me paper?'

Tom took a deep breath and stepped into the small room.

Damp clothes hung on the radiators, causing condensation to run down the windows. The old mantel clock above the electric fire struck four. Dad wiped his chin and cleaned his greasy fingers on his dirty white T-shirt.

'Here,' said Tom, tossing the rolled-up newspaper, which landed with a slap on his dad's large thighs. Dad grunted and took another bite out of his sandwich.

Tom couldn't stand this man, and he hated the way he treated his mum. One day he would get out of this tiny house, taking his mum with him. It wouldn't bother him if he never saw his deadbeat dad again.

Tom rushed his dinner down, then sneaked upstairs, changed into his jeans, pulled a thick jumper over his head and crept down again.

He slipped silently past his dad, who was now snoring, his head back with his mouth wide open.

'Mum, I'm off out with Eve and Clovis. We're just going trick-or-treating.' He hated lying to her, but he didn't think he was really doing anything wrong. He was just going on a little adventure with his best mates and he knew that his dad would never let him go.

'Don't be late, love. You know how he gets if you come in late.'

'I won't, Mum. I'll see you later.' He hugged her then tiptoed quietly out of the house, grabbing his coat and bike.

Clovis knew he was going to be late getting to Eve's as he hadn't even got home and changed yet. Finding the lift had broken down *again*, he'd started the arduous task of climbing the ten flights of stairs to his flat. After what seemed an age, he sighed a heavy sigh of relief as he eventually stepped onto his floor. It was a good job he didn't live on the fifteenth floor, that didn't even bear thinking about.

He passed neighbours chatting and little children playing, and he couldn't help but smile as he got closer to his front door because the smell of Mum's cooking was amazing – and his stomach rumbled in agreement. Her cooking was just the best and Eve and Tom were always asking to come over, especially when they knew she was cooking her famous jerk chicken. Clovis shut the door behind him and heard music playing in the front room. Taking his coat off, he popped his head around the corner and was amazed at the sight before him.

His older brother Jahmeel was dancing in the middle of the room, completely unaware that Clovis had come in. Jahmeel always fancied himself as a bit of a star, but in reality, Clovis thought he looked like someone desperate for the toilet. He tried not to laugh but the scene was too funny and he failed dismally, snorting through his nose.

Jahmeel jumped. 'Bloody hell! You scared me!'

'You scared *me*,' laughed Clovis. 'I thought you were having some sort of fit.'

'Ha, ha,' said Jahmeel, turning down the music. 'How was school?'

'It was good, actually,' said Clovis, taking his glasses off and cleaning them on his jumper.

'Oh, yeah, why? Got a girlfriend yet?' Jahmeel loved to tease his younger brother.

'Nope, but I've got a really interesting homework piece to write about Pagans. Fascinating, did you know, for example—'

'Come on, Einstein,' interrupted Jahmeel, 'Mum's been cooking all day. We've been waiting for you so we can eat.' Jahmeel loved his brother, but sometimes he wished he could just relax and chill out.

The kitchen was steamed up, and a large bowl of different-coloured vegetables swam in a delicious-smelling sauce; potatoes and curries sat in little side dishes.

Claudette Gayle believed in feeding her boys well, because if they were well-fed their brains could work harder. Her two sons were her proudest achievement and she doted on their every need, but she was no pushover. Claudette was in charge of her household and her boys knew it.

'Mum, this looks amazing!' said Clovis. He folded his long lean legs under the small table.

Claudette looked proudly at the feast set before them. The boys piled their plates high and tucked in.

'Mum, remember I'm going out tonight, you said I could,' said Clovis as he dished more scrumptious stew onto his plate.

'Yes, I remember. Are you with Eve and Tom?'

'Yeah, trick-or-treating.' Clovis kept his head down. If his mum or brother saw his face, they would know he was lying.

'I said you could go. But don't be out too late. And make sure your phone is charged,' said Claudette.

'Where are you going?' asked Jahmeel, chasing a juicy pepper round his plate.

'Oh, you know just round the estate.' Clovis kept stabbing at his food, not daring to look up.

'I want you in by ten o'clock at the latest, you hear me, Clovis?' Claudette's voice was sharp and stern.

Clovis finally looked up, glad that his glasses had steamed up so his family couldn't see his eyes. If they knew he was getting the tube to Epping Forest, they would go mad.

'Great, thanks, Mum.' Clovis smiled and continued to shovel food into his lying mouth.

CHAPTER 4

A Haunted House and a Call for Help

The streetlights shone down on the puddled pavements, making everything glow a vibrant golden orange, while the damp streets reflected fireworks exploding in the night sky, transforming the deprived concrete tenements and highlighting the trick-or-treaters who knocked on doors hoping for another handful of sweets.

The three friends were all standing outside Eve's house with their bikes. Clovis and Tom were bundled up in their thick winter coats and both wore beanie hats, determined to keep the cold weather out. Eve insisted her black biker jacket would keep her warm, but the two boys knew she would be sniffling by the end of the night.

'Have you got everything?' asked Tom, his breath swirling and disappearing into the cold night air.

'Yes, a torch each, one camera, and the board,' answered Eve.

'Right then, let's go!' said Clovis, pushing down on his pedal and setting off at a fast pace. After a five-minute bike ride, they arrived at Whitechapel tube station and were just in time to catch the train. They loaded their bikes on and were lucky enough to find seats next to each other.

'What did you tell your mum?' Eve asked Clovis. They all knew he couldn't lie to save his life.

'I said what you told me to say, that we're trick-or-treating,' said Clovis.

'Did she believe you?'

'I think so.'

'I can't wait,' whispered Tom. 'I've always wanted to try a Ouija board. But I'm a bit worried now about what you said, Clovis. What if something evil *does* come through? What if something follows us home?'

'Don't be daft,' whispered back Eve. 'We'll be all right. Nothing happens to the people on the ghost-hunting documentaries, does it? Chances are it won't even work, it's just going to be a laugh. Your problem is you watch too many horror movies.'

'Yeah, she's right, those movies scramble your brain, make you imagine all sorts of weird stuff.' Clovis was about to begin a speech on how the brain reacts to certain images and noise stimuli, but the others knew their friend well and were not in the mood for one of his long-winded scientific ramblings.

Tom cut in quickly before Clovis could get going. 'Want one?' he asked, handing packs of cheese and onion crisps to his friends.

The train rumbled and screeched on for forty-five minutes. Eve, Tom and Clovis chattered happily about their day and what they hoped to experience later. They watched as Halloween party-goers got on and off the train, and they laughed and nudged each other as they saw Frankenstein's monster trying to kiss a zombie, who in turn was attempting to take a drink from a bottle. She failed dismally, spilling it all over the floor and causing a fairy to slip and be picked up by a small hairy gorilla. The mood was a happy one, everyone celebrating much too loudly.

'Next stop,' said Eve, standing up and stumbling slightly as the train jolted abruptly. They all stood in the train carriage watching their reflections as the backdrop of the inky blackness rushed by.

At last the train began to slow down and jerked to a stop. The doors slid open to reveal the station sign *Loughton*, then the tannoy speaker reminded its passengers to 'mind the gap'. Weaving in and out of the party-goers and commuters, Eve, Tom and Clovis pushed their bikes along the Victorian tunnel system until eventually they were standing outside in the cold October air. Now just a short bike ride to Epping Forest, where their adventure really could begin.

The old house apparently stood right in the middle of the forest, alone, derelict and dilapidated; a former shell of what once would have been a beautiful cottage.

The friends sped towards it through the dark forest, chatting and shouting to each other in excitement. They had been riding for ten minutes when Eve suddenly put her brakes on and rummaged in her backpack, pulling out a piece of paper. 'According to Uncle Rufus's notes and sketches, it should be around here somewhere.'

'Well, I can't see anything but trees,' said Tom.

'Yes, but if nobody knows about this place, it's not going to be in plain sight, is it? It will be hidden behind trees or bushes or something,' suggested Clovis.

They put their bikes down, pointing their torches and searching frantically for a clue as to where the house could be.

'There!' Eve shouted eventually, pointing to a clearing in the trees. Everyone came to a stop and followed Eve's torchlight. 'A chimney, I'm sure of it. Can you see it?' Eve's voice was at a whisper, the boys could tell she was excited.

'OK. But are we really sure about this?' asked Clovis, who was by now a little nervous himself. Not only had he lied to his mum and his brother about where he was going, which was bad enough, but if they knew he was about to enter a creepy old house in the middle of Epping Forest to use a Ouija board, they would both completely flip out.

'YES!' shouted Eve over her shoulder, and Clovis muttered to himself as he followed his friends through the thick bracken towards the looming old dilapidated house.

Close up, the house was bigger than the three friends had been expecting and from what they could make out by torchlight, it would once have been an impressive gamekeeper's cottage. But now part of the roof had caved in and the trees and ivy had begun to possess the large front room. Perched high on the building, demonic stone gargoyles sat, crouched as if about to jump on any unsuspecting guests. The gargoyles' tongues protruded out of their beaky mouths, showing their displeasure with anyone who happened to be paying a visit.

'Very charming, I'm sure,' said Eve as her torch lit up a gargoyle who seemed to be staring straight at her.

'Shall we go in then?' asked Tom.

'After you,' Clovis said, moving aside to let his best friend go first.

'No, after *you*,' replied Tom, a smile spreading across his face.

'Oh, for God's sake you two,' said Eve, pushing past them. 'I'll go first, you idiots. Anyone would think you were *scared*.' She then began to do an impression of a chicken, clucking and flapping her arms about.

All of a sudden, a fox cried out and the flutter of a bird moving in a nearby tree made them all scream.

'It's all right, it's all right, only the wildlife,' laughed Clovis, who was trying to relax a bit by thinking logical thoughts.

Once inside, the group decided to base themselves in what would once have been the living room. Now, old lager cans, rubbish, rubble and wood littered the floor. It was cold, and the room smelled of mould and damp.

In no time, Eve had set up the night-vision camera on a small tripod in the corner, making sure that the whole room was in shot.

'Never mind the dead, do you think *we'll* be all right?

I mean, what if we come across someone alive?' asked Tom, as he began to clear a space for them to sit down. 'What if somebody is living rough in here?'

'Well it doesn't look like anyone's been here for a very long time,' said Eve. 'Look, this newspaper is over fifteen years old. I think we'll be OK.'

'Right,' said Tom. 'Put the Ouija board here in the middle. Leave your torch on, Eve, and let's promise each other that no one pushes the glass.'

'We'd be a bit stupid to do that,' said Clovis. 'It's taken us ages to get here. That's a lot of time wasted for one of us to just mess about.'

'All right, point taken. I was just saying . . .' pouted Tom.

'Right, let's do this,' whispered Eve, 'before we talk ourselves out of it.' Rubbing her cold hands together, her eyes sparkled with excitement in the torchlight. She couldn't believe they were actually about to do this. If her uncle Rufus found out, he would be so disappointed in her, but he *wasn't* going to find out, surely. This was their secret and as long as no one said a word, there would be no need for any of their parents to know.

The little drinking glass was set upside down in the centre of the board. The alphabet letters curved across the middle and numbers sat in a line running along the bottom. One word was written on each of the four corners: *Yes* and *No* at either end of the bottom, and *Hello* and *Goodbye* at either end of the top.

'OK, so who wants to ask it a question?' giggled Tom nervously.

'I will,' said Clovis. His face was serious as he bent forward and placed his finger on the upturned glass. The others followed his lead.

'Is anybody there?' Clovis's voice was firm and steady. His glasses had fallen to the end of his nose and his brow was furrowed in deep concentration.

Eve and Tom looked at each other, excited yet scared at the same time.

'Is there anybody there? If there is, move the glass.' Clovis's voice was getting louder, more commanding. Suddenly, the glass jumped.

'Whoa!' cried Tom, snatching his finger away.

'What the hell!' shouted Eve.

'Put your fingers back on, I'm sure this is just micro-muscular movement. It's just our energies making it move. Don't worry, it's fine.'

Clovis had a calming effect on his friends.

'How come you seem to know so much about all this?' asked Eve.

'You know me,' replied Clovis, looking a little embarrassed. 'I did my research, that's all.'

'Go on then, keep talking. It's working, whatever you're doing,' said Tom, staring hard at the board.

All of a sudden a huge bang exploded above them. It sounded as though something had fallen onto the floor upstairs.

'Oh my God, what the hell was that?' shouted Eve, jumping to her feet. 'Maybe we should go. I don't think this was such a good idea.'

'Don't be daft, Eve, it's just the wind,' said Clovis, pulling on her arm to get her to sit down again.

Sure enough, as if on cue, a gust of wind suddenly howled through the old building, and the trees could now be heard to creak and moan. And then a *tap, tap, tap* noise came from behind them.

'What's that?' Tom screamed, twisting his body round to look behind him. He clicked his torch on and scanned the room.

Eve sprang up again like a nervous cat and shrieked, 'Tom, for God's sake . . . you're scaring the crap out of me.'

'Look, guys, will you both get a grip,' said Clovis. 'It's a tree branch tapping on the window. Remember there's usually a logical explanation to most things.'

Eve and Tom sighed out in relief. Clovis grabbed Eve's hands again and pulled her back once more to the Ouija board.

'You're right, sorry, guys,' laughed Eve. 'OK, Clovis, ask again.'

Clovis cleared his throat and began to call out again to any spirits who might be around. And once more, slowly but surely, the glass began to move.

'Oh, my God! It's moving!' whispered Tom.

'Keep it together, guys,' said Clovis calmly. 'Don't break the circle. Can you tell us your name?' he asked the board.

'If this glass spells a name out, I think I will die,' whispered Tom.

The glass began to move more steadily now, round and round in a circle. The noise it made scraping along the wooden board was one of the creepiest sounds Tom had ever heard. Then just as suddenly as the glass had started to move, it stopped.

The wind outside was getting louder, the trees bent and groaning. Eve shivered in the dark room; her face was illuminated by the soft glow of the torchlight.

'Shall we leave?' she asked. 'I don't mind admitting it, I'm really scared now. This is way spookier than I imagined.'

'We can't go yet,' moaned Tom. 'We've only just got started.'

'It's all right, Eve,' said Clovis. 'Nothing bad is going to happen. This is just a piece of wood, remember. I don't think it's going to summon up the Devil.'

'But you said sometimes evil ghosts can come through.'

'Yes, I know I said that, but really we've got no reason to believe that an evil dead person is trying to speak to us, have we?'

They still had their fingers on the glass, and all of them screamed as it suddenly began to move again. But none of them let go. This time the glass moved towards the alphabet. One by one it rolled over the letters, stopping at different ones in turn, then moving to another. First an *H*, then an *E*, followed by an *L* and a *P*.

'*HELP ME*,' spelled out Clovis.

Tom and Eve took big gulps and looked nervously at each other.

'Who are you? Tell us your name,' demanded Clovis.

The glass started to glide across the board once more.

'*C . . . O . . . M . . . E T . . . O M . . . E*,' spelled out Eve. Again, the letters were making sense.

'Where? Where shall we find you?' Eve's voice was very quiet, not quite believing what she was witnessing.

The glass moved again; this time it was much quicker. Jerky violent thrusts shunted it at high speed across the board, as if whoever they were talking to was in a hurry, desperate to get the information out.

The glass spelled out the word *BELOW*.

'Below?' queried Tom, looking at his friends in confusion. 'What does that mean?'

The glass moved slower now, rolling over the letters to spell out the word *PLEASE*. It picked up speed and moved over more letters: *DON'T GO*. Then it began to slide across the board as if in anger. It went so fast, the friends had trouble keeping their fingers on top of it. They pressed down hard but it seemed to have a life of its own, and without warning the glass flew off the board, violently spun through the air and smashed against the wall.

Suddenly the banging noises started again from above. Eve, Tom and Clovis stood up and held onto each other, terrified.

As if things couldn't get any more frightening, Tom now pointed upwards to the ceiling. The noise was beginning to sound like steady, heavy footsteps echoing through the empty house: slow, menacing and precise.

'Someone's up there,' whispered Tom in a shaky voice.

'Shush!' said Eve, looking upwards.

They all fixed their eyes onto the ceiling and followed the noise with pointed fingers. It seemed to be going towards the top of the stairs.

'I'll go and check. It could be anything,' said Clovis.

The footsteps continued, then a disturbing dragging noise could be heard.

'Are you mad?' hissed Tom.

'We need to check that no one is up there, playing tricks on us,' insisted Clovis.

'And what if there is?' replied Tom.

'Yeah, what then?' said Eve.

'We have to check. If we don't, we'll never know if someone human is messing with us, or whether there's the possibility that this place is actually haunted.'

Tom and Eve knew that Clovis was right and that he wouldn't give up until he got his way and explored all possibilities.

With a sigh, Tom agreed. 'I can't believe we are about to do this.'

'Neither can I,' said Eve. 'I suppose you're right, though.'

Clovis led the way slowly up the crumbling staircase. Eve

followed in the middle as she didn't want to be at the back and Tom brought up the rear with the camera.

Clovis's torch lit the narrow staircase, revealing more rubbish, creeping ivy and cobwebs. Turning right, they shuffled into the doorway of the room they had heard the noises coming from.

'Well there's no one in *here*,' said Tom, panning the night-vision camera all around the room.

'And it would be very difficult for anyone to walk about up here, as there don't seem to be many floorboards left,' said Clovis.

Tom let out a sigh. 'I just don't know what to make of it all.'

'I know, me neither, but we all heard those noises. They were definitely footsteps,' said Eve, shivering and hugging herself.

'Well, it's confused me,' said Clovis. 'I just don't understand—'

But as he was about to start one of his scientific monologues, he was interrupted by a man's raised whisper that growled throughout the house.

'HELP ME!'

All three friends screamed and ran as quickly as they could down the stairs, pushing past each other, all trying to be the first out and gain as much distance between themselves and whatever had called out.

'Quick, get out. Get out!' screamed Eve.

In the confusion and panic, Tom and Clovis fell over each other, and both landed hard at the foot of the stairs.

'Ow, Clovis, watch where you're going. Quick, grab the board and let's get out of here!' cried Tom.

Clovis grabbed their stuff and they ran to their bikes. Once on them, they rode as fast as their legs could pedal. Only when they reached the tube station did they stop to catch their breaths. And no one said a word until they were back on the train, where they whispered quietly to each other, running through what they had all just encountered, each of them trying to process what they had witnessed.

They arrived back at Whitechapel just before ten o'clock, relieved, tired and confused. 'We say nothing to anybody about this.' Eve glared at her two friends. They were all standing outside Eve's house.

'Agreed, I need to get some sleep. And I need to analyse what happened,' said Clovis.

'Let's meet tomorrow. You guys come here; we'll have the house to ourselves. Uncle Rufus is out for lunch at the university,' said Eve.

'OK, great,' said Tom. 'I've got football training in the morning, so I'll come straight over after that. We need to watch the footage back.'

'Remember not a word,' said Eve. 'Wow! What a night. See you tomorrow and, guys . . . Happy Halloween!'

CHAPTER 5

The Evidence Speaks for Itself

Eve was back in the haunted house. The dark, damp walls began to move, expanding and retracting as if they were breathing. The pounding noise was deafening, and blood began to drip from the ceiling. *Drip, drip, drip*, it splashed onto her forehead. *BANG! BANG!* The noise was getting louder, the wet sticky blood now all over her face. She began to scream out to Tom and Clovis, but no one answered, just a tapping sound in her ears, over and over again. Screaming, she woke and sat bolt upright in bed, trying to catch her breath. She took huge gulps of air, attempting to calm herself down, and looked wildly round the room searching for anything familiar, to prove she had escaped a nightmare and was back in the real world.

Seeing Boris lying on her bed, her posters on the wall, Mum and Dad's picture smiling down at her, she pulled herself together, got out of bed and opened the curtains. The afternoon sun came streaming in and instantly she felt better. Boris's sticky saliva was on her face and someone was banging at the front door.

Thankfully it had just been a bad dream, but then the memories of last night came rushing back to her. It's true she had been petrified but now, in the daylight, she also felt intrigued. Last night had been truly insane.

Eve quickly put on some jeans and a jumper and then ran down the stairs. Boris followed eagerly and began to bark in excitement.

'I'm coming!' she shouted, as she padded down the long corridor. On the side table by the front door there was a note from Uncle Rufus.

Darling girl, hope you had a nice lie in. See you later. Love Unc x
P.S. Don't eat the cheese, I think it's going off.

Eve opened the heavy door. An icy blast of cold air rushed in, causing her to grab both her friends and drag them inside.

Boris was beside himself with excitement and began barking again, jumping up at Clovis and Tom, wiggling his bottom with sheer joy. Everyone went to the kitchen and began to rifle through the cupboards and the fridge. Tom and Clovis knew where everything was kept and treated Eve's home as if it were their own. Bread was put into the toaster; the kettle was switched on and three mugs were lined up ready to be filled with hot chocolate.

Eve sat down at the kitchen table, yawned and scratched her head. Her short blonde hair stuck up at odd angles, and her pretty blue eyes still looked heavy with sleep. Tom and Clovis were leaning on the countertop, both looked dishevelled and exhausted. Clovis had red eyes and was wearing the same clothes he'd worn yesterday. Tom was still in his football training gear. Mud had dried on the knees of his tracksuit bottoms, his hair was sticking up and flecks of dirt were speckled on his face.

While they waited for the bread to toast, they began to talk about what they had witnessed the night before.

'Or what we *think* we witnessed,' added Clovis.

'Hang on, Clovis, let me get this straight,' said Eve. 'Are you saying that *wasn't* a ghost? That there is a logical explanation for the glass moving on its own, then smashing against the wall?' She stood up and began to pace the floor, exasperated with her friend.

'And what about the footsteps, the banging and—' Tom added.

'And let's not forget the voice we ALL heard,' interrupted Eve, beginning to shout. Sometimes Clovis's scientific brain really got on her nerves.

'All I'm saying is that we mustn't rush to conclusions,' said Clovis. The toaster popped and he leaned over and grabbed two pieces of toast and began to butter them.

'Come on, Eve,' said Tom. 'Don't get angry. Let's go into the front room and watch the footage. We might have caught something else that may convince Einstein here.' He prodded Clovis in the ribs and pinched the toast out of his hand just as he was about to take a big bite.

The three friends took their food and moved into the front room. It was the most lived-in room in the house. A battered old sofa took precedence in the centre, hundreds of books lined the walls from floor to ceiling, and books that couldn't fit on the shelves were stacked in neat piles all around the room. Unusual objects littered every bit of spare space. An old telescope, a crystal ball, old poison bottles, shells from some far-off distant paradise. Eve's uncle had travelled the world for most of his life and had made it a rule to always come back with a treasure or two. Eve's favourite was an old Egyptian jewellery box that he had brought back for her. It was ancient, and according to her uncle, 'a rare find indeed'.

Uncle Rufus had laid a fire before he went out and they soon had it crackling and hissing in the grate and giving off a reddish glow. The toast and hot chocolate were going down nicely and the calming effect of that and the cosy room seemed to mellow everyone's mood.

'I'm sorry, Clovis . . . you know, about before,' said Eve. 'It's just I had a bad night. I've hardly slept and I had a terrifying nightmare this morning.'

'Snap!' said Tom.

'Me too,' added Clovis.

'What was your dream about?' asked Tom, looking at Eve.

'I was back in that awful house. The walls were breathing

and there was blood everywhere. It was horrific. What about you guys?'

'Basically the same as yours,' replied Tom.

'And you, Clovis?' asked Eve.

'Yes, the same,' he mumbled. 'I woke up on the floor shouting with my duvet wrapped around me. Mum came in, she was really worried.'

'That can't be a coincidence, surely?' said Tom.

'Maybe,' said Clovis. 'I have to admit that for all three of us to have had the same dream does seem very unusual.'

The three friends sat in silence, not really knowing what to make of this new piece of information. Clovis's laptop interrupted their thoughts by beeping to let them know that the footage had been uploaded from the camera and was ready to be watched. Clovis put the laptop on his knees and the others leaned in close.

'Right, here we go,' he said, hitting the play button.

The footage showed everything in black and white, and the room in the haunted house looked so clear. They could see things now that they hadn't been able to last night — a small broken chair in the corner, empty bookshelves on the walls.

They watched in silence, living out the whole frightening scenario again, the sound of the glass moving, the wind howling, the bang upstairs. Then suddenly, Tom jumped up, crying loudly, 'Stop it! Stop!' He clicked the space bar and took a deep breath. 'Take the footage back to the part where Eve sits down the second time.'

Clovis slid the cursor back to the right place, then before he pressed play, Tom leaned closer to the screen.

'Look about here.' Tom pointed to the corner of the room on the screen. 'Now press play.'

Clovis pressed the space bar. All three leaned in close, then suddenly recoiled back in horror.

'Oh my God!' hissed Eve.

'Look at it!' shouted Tom.

'Now hang on just a minute, let's look again,' said Clovis.

Over and over, Tom, Eve and Clovis watched the footage. And there was no doubt about it. They could see what looked like a black shadow slowly emerging from the back wall, creeping slowly, growing in size with every second. The dark object was moving towards the three of them, inky black tendrils reaching out, feeling its way across the floor. The terrifying shadow seemed to be morphing into a human shape. It looked vaguely like a man but then it changed shape again, moving towards Clovis, surrounding him, covering his head and shoulders. The shape then turned its attention to Tom, slithering towards him in a snake-like motion. It looked as if it were studying him, its elongated fingers covering his face, stroking his head. Moving once more, it crawled towards Eve but this time as she screamed, the black smog entered her mouth, disappearing for just a second before it slid back out, emerging from her nostrils. The blackness then hovered over the Ouija board and as soon as the banging and footsteps were heard upstairs it just disappeared, vanishing back into the darkness.

'What the hell!' Eve's face was practically squashed against the screen.

'It's definitely not a shadow,' said Clovis, more to himself than to his friends. His face was scrunched up in furious concentration.

'Of course it's not. It's a ghost!' shouted Tom. 'I'm telling you, that freaky weird thing is a ghost, it can't be anything else.' He was shouting now, his voice getting more and more high pitched. He was scared by what he had just seen, but also incredibly excited. 'I can't believe what we've caught,' he continued, talking at a million words an hour. 'This thing could go viral; this could be huge!'

Tom was standing on the sofa now and Boris was becoming very excited and began to bark.

Eve stood up and started to pace the floor, nearly falling over Boris. 'We can't do anything yet,' she said. 'I think we need to wait for a bit.'

'Why?' asked Tom, sounding like a whiny child.

'Because,' said Clovis, 'if we post this online, our parents, Uncle Rufus, my brother – they will all know what we did and where we went last night.'

'They will all know we lied,' continued Eve, 'and I for one don't fancy being grounded.'

'No, and I don't want my laptop and phone taken off me,' said Clovis.

Deflated, Tom sat back down again. 'Oh, I hadn't thought of that,' he said, biting his thumb distractedly.

'I think Eve's right, let's wait a bit so we can come up with a plan. Then when we do post the footage out there, we can have our story straight,' said Clovis, putting his laptop in his bag.

'But that still doesn't answer the question. What *was* that thing? And who were we talking to on the board?' said Tom.

'I don't want to talk about that thing coming out of my nostrils,' said Eve, shuddering. 'Makes me go cold just thinking about it.'

'I have to watch the footage again,' said Clovis, 'and I need to check that the camera isn't damaged in any way as it was very damp in there. We have to make sure that what we have just seen isn't a naturally occurring error or a technical flaw. But what I find fascinating is that we all dreamed the same thing last night. I'm going to do some more research when I get home.'

There was a long pause, interrupted by the front door banging shut. Eve, Tom and Clovis all jumped. Boris leaped up from his prostrate position and snuffled off to meet his master.

'Hello, you guys! What you up to?' Uncle Rufus stood in the doorway, unwinding his extraordinary long scarf from around his neck.

'Oh, hi,' answered Eve. 'We were just talking about some

homework,' she said, trying to sound convincing though she knew she looked flustered.

'Mmm, I'm not convinced,' said Uncle Rufus, rubbing his chin. 'You boys staying for dinner? I thought pizza.'

'Ah thanks, Professor, but I have to get back home. My mum's got me and Jahmeel doing some chores,' said Clovis, smiling up at his hero.

'Yeah, me too,' said Tom standing up. 'I'd love to stay but you know what my dad's like. It's the match tomorrow. Early night . . . you know.'

Tom and Clovis put their coats on. Eve went with them to the front door, where they whispered their goodbyes and promised each other not to say a word about last night or the footage. Once the door was closed, Eve walked into the kitchen to find Uncle Rufus with his head in the fridge.

'So, what was all that whispering about?' he mumbled.

'Oh, nothing. I didn't realise we *were* whispering,' said Eve. 'Uncle, can I ask you something?' She sat down and began to fiddle with the tablecloth.

'Anything, dear girl.' Uncle Rufus emerged from the fridge with a carrot in his mouth, which he promptly bit into with a satisfying crunch.

'Do you believe in ghosts?'

'Er . . . well, I suppose . . . I'd have to say . . . yes,' said Uncle Rufus, pulling out a chair to sit opposite his niece. 'Do you?'

'I think I do, yes, but the thought of them terrifies me.'

'I know what you mean. The first time I saw your Aunt Jess, I—'

Eve interrupted him. 'What do you mean, Uncle?' Leaning forward, she whispered, 'Are you saying you've seen her *ghost*?'

She was stunned, never expecting to hear that. Uncle Rufus was a scientist, a man of logic, he didn't believe in Halloween and 'all that poppycock'. And when she'd asked him about the haunted cottage in the photo the day after she'd found it, he'd laughed and dismissed it as a typical urban myth. And now he was telling her that he'd seen a ghost?

'Oh, I *thought* I saw her,' Uncle Rufus said, suddenly looking sad. 'But it was probably only a dream. It was just after she died, and I was so desperate to see her. I kept talking out loud, asking her to come and pay me a visit, but in the end, well, I just fell asleep and that's when I saw her. But I'm sure there's a logical explanation to most things, including ghosts.'

Eve wanted to tell her uncle what they had done last night and show him the freaky footage, but she was afraid he would be angry with her. The last thing she wanted to do was let him down, they only had each other in this world, and she wasn't about to disappoint him.

'Come on,' said Uncle Rufus, changing the subject. 'Let's go get some pizza. It's a Saturday night. We'll eat together in front of the TV and watch one of those silly movies you like so much.'

Uncle Rufus, Eve and Boris walked out of the house, blissfully unaware that something supernatural had entered their home uninvited, and was about to change their lives for ever.

CHAPTER 6

The Face in the TV

Tom's house was small. It had two bedrooms, a basic kitchen and a front room. When Tom was little, he hadn't noticed how compact it was but now he felt trapped, claustrophobic and uneasy. His dad, Dan, had never really been interested in him. Only when Tom had learned to kick a football had Dad sat up and taken some notice of him. The two had nothing in common apart from football and Tom's mum. Communication between the two of them was a mix of hand gestures, grunts, nods and the odd smile. And it had pretty much been like that all of Tom's life. All he had ever wanted was for a dad who was proud of him. Only on very rare occasions would Dad leave the security of his worn-out armchair and join the other red-faced parents on the side-lines of an important football match that Tom was playing in. Dad would shuffle up and down the pitch, his little legs going as fast as they could. He would scream and bellow coaching tips above the other parents for his son to hear. All of Tom's teammates liked their parents coming to watch a match but Tom dreaded it. He was embarrassed by his dad.

Dad didn't really pay Tom much attention but when he did Tom just wanted to curl up and die.

Each day it felt as though Tom were counting down the hours till he could leave his home — whether it be going to school, football or to visit Clovis and Eve. He just couldn't stand to be near his dad, despite how much he loved his mum.

Tom lay in his bed looking up at the ceiling. It was late, and he was wide awake. He just didn't feel sleepy. His gaze followed the car headlights as they moved across the walls, highlighting his West Ham posters. He could hear his dad's regular thunderous snores, undulating in pitch then pausing for a few seconds only to start up again like a spluttering old pig in the last throes of its life.

Tom looked at his clock, its orange numbers illuminated the small bedroom: *12:45 am*.

Why couldn't he sleep? Maybe he was afraid to. After last night's nightmare, he wasn't surprised. He didn't want another one of those. Restless, with his brain a whirr, he began to go over the frightening video footage they had recorded again. Now, he was one hundred per cent convinced that ghosts *did* exist, but was one trying to get their attention?

Suddenly, he sat up, aware of voices coming from the front room. He got out of bed and pressed his ear to the door, straining to hear who was talking, but he didn't recognise who it was. Then he realised it was just the TV. Had his dad gone into the front room to watch something? That would be unusual, because once that man was asleep, nothing could wake him. Maybe it was his mum, thought Tom. He grabbed his jumper and opened the bedroom door. The volume of the TV was getting louder and louder. What was going on? He hurried into the front room, expecting to see either his mum or dad sitting on the sofa watching a late-night film, but there was no one there. He looked around for the remote control, but it had seemingly disappeared.

'What the hell is going on?' boomed his dad. He stood in the doorway; his pyjama bottoms slightly askew, pushed down on one side by his enormous bulbous stomach. Mum stood behind him, looking confused, and placed her hands over her ears in an attempt to blank out the loud booming noises coming from the TV. She stared in astonishment at Tom, accusing him with no words.

'Turn that bloody thing off, Tom!' shouted his dad, lumbering forward into the room. Instantly Tom pressed the button on the TV, but nothing happened. His dad nudged him out the way and began pressing the button himself like a frenzied child on a computer game desperate to win points. Still nothing happened, in fact the opposite seemed to occur. The more Dad pressed the button, the louder the noise from the TV became.

Dad rolled his eyes and screamed at Tom, 'Get the plug!'

So, Tom got down on his hands and knees and shuffled under the TV stand. The film being shown was an old black and white movie that was now in the midst of a car chase, police sirens and a Chicago mafia shootout. The noise was deafening.

Tom pulled the plug and expected the room to go silent, but it did no such thing.

'What the hell are you playing at?' Dad was hysterical and sweat had begun to glisten on his brow. Now the front doorbell chimed several times, signalling that someone was waiting impatiently at the door. Ange ran quickly up the hallway, clutching at her nightdress as she went to open it.

Tom shuffled backwards from under the TV with the plug in his hand. He was astounded. The TV should have stopped working, what on Earth was happening? Showing the plug to his dad, he shrugged his shoulders.

'Quick, get your duvet, cover the TV with it, that might muffle the sound a bit.'

Tom did just as his dad suggested. It did help a bit but not enough and it wasn't long before half a dozen neighbours showed up in the front room, some half asleep but all complaining about the noise. They proceeded to give advice as to how to shut the TV off.

Tom watched on and almost smiled at the absurdity of it all. People he had known for most of his life were standing in his home in their pyjamas and dressing gowns. Mrs Jessop who lived next door was wearing some sort of fluffy onesie, complete with huge bunny ears.

Dad repeatedly showed them that the television *wasn't*

plugged in. He seemed to be enjoying the attention, Tom thought, that was until the police barged in.

They'd received a complaint of a loud disturbance on the estate. Several officers arrived on the scene and burst through the doors. When they realised that the noises were coming from a large TV and that the crowd of people in the flat were not there for a party but to complain about the noise, they looked relieved.

'Who lives here?' a police officer bellowed over the din.

Dad and Mum raised their hands.

'Right, turn that TV off right now, and the rest of you can go home.'

'I can't,' mouthed Dad and again he held the plug up to prove that the TV wasn't even plugged in.

The baffled police officers decided to take the TV away, as it was causing too much noise and commotion. But just as two officers were about to lift it off its stand, the screen suddenly turned to black, and the noise died. Everyone began to talk at once, complaining and telling Dan and Ange to get their electrical equipment sorted out. The police ushered the angry mob out of the house and ordered Tom's family not to put the TV on again that night.

When everyone was gone and all was quiet, Tom and his parents sank onto the sofa in relief.

'What the hell was that all about?' asked his dad. 'Have you been messing with it?' he said to Tom.

'Of course not,' said Tom defensively. 'It woke me up too.'

'You sure you didn't fiddle with a button or something?' asked Dad, still not convinced.

'I *swear*. I didn't touch the TV.' Tom was getting upset now. Why did his dad blame everything that went wrong on him?

'I believe you, Tom,' said his mum, putting a protective arm around her son's shoulders. 'One thing Tom isn't, is a liar, Dan, you know that.'

At that moment the TV turned itself back on again. Tom and his parents leaped back from it as if they had been electrocuted. Black static rained on the screen and a deep growling voice seemed to be coming from within.

'It looks like a *face*,' said Mum.

'Shhhh, it's saying something,' said Dad.

The three of them listened in silence. Mum held Tom's hand tightly.

'What's it saying?' she whispered. 'Oh my God, it's saying—'

'Help me,' finished Tom. He stood up and placed his hands on the screen, staring into what looked like the outline of a man's face.

Then just as quickly as the TV had come on, it died again.

Mum looked like a frightened rabbit caught in the glare of a car's headlights. An eerie silence filled the little house.

Tom shuddered. He knew this had something to do with what happened last night. But he daren't tell his mum and dad, they would go mad.

'*Shush*,' whispered Dad. He cocked his head to one side. 'Can you hear that?'

'Hear what?' asked Mum, looking quizzically at her husband.

'It sounds like someone flicking a light switch on and off.'

'I can hear it,' said Tom.

The three of them rushed into the hall. Sure enough the light above their heads was flicking on and off. But what made it scarier was that they could all see and hear the light switch at the far end of the hall moving up and down on its own.

'This has got to be some sort of prank,' said Dad, nervously sliding down the hallway with his back to the wall. Ange and Tom were holding onto each other and following him. As soon as they got to the light switch—

BANG! All the lights in the house went out.

'Arghh!' shouted Dad.

'Dan!' squealed back Mum.

'Get a torch, Tom, quick!'

Tom blindly bumbled up to his bedroom, grabbed his phone and put the torch on. Making his way back to his parents, he saw that his dad had his arm around Mum's shoulders, and she looked as if she might burst into tears at any moment.

'I think it may be an electrical surge, Dad,' said Tom, handing his phone to him.

'You're probably right, mate, or a blown fuse. Open the fuse box, let's have a look.'

Tom and Dad got down on their knees and opened up the fuse box hidden inside the hall cupboard.

Tom held the lid up and Dad grunted, breathing heavily as he shone a light on each fuse.

'Ah ha!' Dad cried. 'There's the little sod. The reason for tonight's nightmare, I reckon . . . the fuse has tripped.' He flicked a switch and to everyone's relief, all the lights came back on.

'Right, everyone, back to bed. I think that's enough excitement for one night.' Dad ruffled Tom's hair in relief.

'You sure?' said Mum surprisingly. 'I thought maybe it was a ghost or something.'

Her husband just laughed. 'Don't be daft, love. There's no such thing as ghosts.'

Tom climbed back into bed. He knew in his gut that it wasn't a faulty fuse that had caused all the commotion tonight. There was something about that voice coming from the TV which had scared him.

'Help me!'

Exactly the same words spelled out by the Ouija board. Tom shivered again in the dark and pulled the duvet up over his head. Was something with him in his room *now*? He was convinced that after last night's excursion to the haunted house he had brought something back with him. Something that was now haunting his home. It was no faulty wiring that had flicked the hall switch on and off. Mum was right, it was a ghost.

Tom sat up in his bed and quickly switched on his bedside lamp. Looking about his small room and seeing the familiar everyday objects all in their right places seemed oddly comforting. He could hear his dad's snoring once more and he placed his earphones in and turned his music up on his phone. Slowly his eyes began to close, exhaustion taking over.

CHAPTER 7

Bloody Footprints

Ring, ring! Ring, ring! The old-fashioned telephone in the hallway rang shrilly in the Gayles' flat. Claudette Gayle, Clovis's mum, only used it for emergencies. The whole family knew only to ring the landline if it were a life-or-death situation.

Clovis's mum's bedroom door flew open first. She leaped on top of the phone like a snake striking its prey. Picking up the receiver, she whispered into it, 'Hello . . . hello, who's there?'

Jahmeel came into the dark hallway, followed closely by Clovis, both boys yawning and scratching their heads.

Mum's voice was becoming angry. 'Now you listen, I can hear you breathing down the phone!'

'Give it to me,' commanded Jahmeel, being the older brother and the designated man of the house. Mum handed the phone to her son.

'Hello, who is this please?' he enquired, using his best deep voice. 'I can hear you . . . I can hear your breathing.'

'Let me have a listen,' said Clovis, impatiently taking the

phone off his brother. 'It could be someone from Jamaica. Maybe the line isn't clear at their end either.' Clovis put his ear to the device and listened. There was an eerie crackling, whistling noise.

'Hello, hello?' he said.

'Hang up,' instructed Mum.

Clovis did what his mum asked and the three of them went back to their rooms, closing their doors behind them.

Ring, ring! Ring, ring!

All three bedroom doors burst open again. This time everyone was completely wide awake.

Mum grabbed the phone again and shouted down the offending mouthpiece.

'Hello!' She was angry now. Her eyes bulged in the dim light. She wasn't being polite any more.

Clovis and Jahmeel started to worry. Their grandparents lived in Jamaica and refused to have a mobile phone, so when the landline *did* ring, it was always Mamma or Pops wanting a chat. No one else had this number, and who in the UK would be calling them at three o'clock in the morning?

'Here, Mum, let me,' said Jahmeel. 'Mamma? Pops? Is that you?' Just more heavy breathing. 'OK, listen, you, whoever you are: stop calling. If you don't, I'll make it my job to find you and then you'll be sorry.' Jahmeel slammed the phone down.

'I'm going to unplug it, Mum,' said Clovis, kneeling down and pulling the little plug from the phone socket.

Mum was busy calling her parents on her mobile in Jamaica. It was ten o'clock at night there. She had to check that her family was OK.

'Hello, Ma! It's me. Have you been trying to call me? You haven't?' Mum looked relieved and rolled her eyes at her two sons. 'Yes, OK, yes I know it's three in the morning here. I'll call you later, Ma. No, we are all fine. I'll explain later today. Love you, bye.'

She clicked her mobile off. 'Well that's good, everybody's fine. Come on, let's all get back to bed. It must have been some kids messing about making prank calls.'

Mum, Clovis and Jahmeel all whispered their goodnights, and made for their bedrooms. Mum, however stopped in her tracks. She picked her bare foot up off the floor: she felt some gooey liquid on the sole.

Flicking on the hall light, she screamed.

Clovis and Jahmeel rushed to her. Their mum's eyes were wide with fear and she didn't speak, just pointed. On the floor, six large blood-red footprints were spaced out as if someone had walked down the hallway and out through the front door. The prints were of bare feet. The outline of the heel and the toes were clear to see.

Clovis gulped and Jahmeel immediately stood protectively in front of his mum.

'Get the baseball bat, Clovis,' whispered Jahmeel.

Clovis did as his brother asked and retrieved the bat from

the broom cupboard in the kitchen. When he came back into the hallway, Jahmeel was looking closely at the prints.

'They go out the front door,' he said.

'And they're fresh,' observed Clovis, bending down to take a closer look too.

'Have either of you cut yourselves?' asked Mum, trying hard to keep composed. The boys quickly checked their feet and shook their heads in confusion. Claudette Gayle was a logical, intelligent woman, but seeing dark, red footprints in the hallway at three o'clock in the morning would make the bravest of people feel very anxious.

Clovis went to the front door, slid the chain out and unbolted it. Opening it slightly, he looked down to see if the footprints were present on the concrete outside, but there was nothing.

'All clear out there,' he said, shutting the door and the cold out behind him.

'Is it paint or blood?' asked Mum nervously, wringing her hands.

Clovis dipped his finger in the red liquid.

'Ergh.' Jahmeel's face scrunched up in disgust, not quite believing his brother could do such a thing, but Clovis was not your usual thirteen-year-old.

Clovis brought his red-tipped index finger slowly up to his nose and sniffed. The metallic smell was strong and evident.

'It's definitely blood, Mum. It's not congealed yet, so whoever walked through our hallway did so very recently.'

'I think we should call the police,' said Mum. Just as she was about to punch *999* into her mobile, the loud ringing noise of the landline ripped through the flat once more.

Everyone jumped and screamed out loud, staring in horror at the vibrating phone sitting innocently on the hall table.

'That shouldn't be happening,' shouted Clovis, over the din. He kneeled down and picked up the end of the telephone's cable, showing his family that it still wasn't plugged back in.

'Something bad is playing with us,' said his mum, shaking her head from side to side. 'This is too much and I don't like it.' She pulled her dressing gown tightly about her body, trying to comfort herself.

Jahmeel snatched up the phone receiver. 'Hello!' he shouted. Again, the same weird, eerie crackling and whistling sound resonated down the line. 'It's the same noise; here, you listen.' Jahmeel thrust the phone into Clovis's hand.

He pushed his glasses up to the bridge of his nose and nervously placed the phone to his ear. Static noise crackled and whistled. Clovis said nothing, just stood quite still waiting for a noise, a voice, anything that could satisfy his logical brain.

Then he heard it.

It was a whisper, a man's voice sounding far off in the distance, then slowly beginning to get louder and louder.

'Help me!' the voice boomed in Clovis's ear. It was loud

and desperate. Clovis didn't move a muscle. He was frozen to the spot with terror.

When the phone had first rung, he'd thought it could be Tom pranking him, but this voice didn't sound anything like Tom, and in his heart Clovis knew that his best friend wouldn't and couldn't do something like this.

As Clovis held onto the phone, the man's voice became even louder. He was shouting desperately now, the same thing over and over. 'Help me, please. Help me!' Then the line went dead.

With a shaking hand, Clovis placed the phone back in its cradle.

'Well?' asked Jahmeel. 'Did you hear anything?'

Clovis looked at his mum and wanted to shout out what he had just heard, but he knew that he couldn't. It would scare her to death, and he didn't want to do that, he could see that she was upset and frightened enough as it was.

'No, just the same thing, crackling and static.'

They all went into the kitchen and Clovis sat down at the table next to his mum, sitting on his hands to stop them from shaking.

He watched as his brother made them all a hot drink.

'I'm asking you both now and I'm expecting an honest answer.' Mum glared at both her sons. 'Have either of you been doing something you shouldn't?'

'Like what, Mum?' asked Jahmeel, stirring sugar into the mugs of steaming hot tea.

'You know — drugs, meeting bad people, anything . . . oh, I don't know.' Mum put her head in her hands. She looked up and Jahmeel and Clovis were shocked to see that she had tears in her eyes.

'Oh, Mum,' said Clovis, putting his arm round her.

'It's all right, Mum,' said Jahmeel. 'It's probably just kids messing about.' He rubbed her back with one hand and placed her mug of tea in front of her with the other.

'I reckon the phone has an electrical fault, and even unplugged it still has enough energy to work, hey, Clovis?' Jahmeel looked at his brother and slyly winked, hoping Clovis would pick up the hint. 'And as for the footprints, I think I might have stepped on a pin earlier tonight and my foot must have bled when I was locking up for the night. Sounds logical, right, Clovis?' Jahmeel stared hard at his brother across the table.

'Well,' began Clovis, taking a sip of the hot sweet tea, 'I'm not entirely sure that a telephone would work if it wasn't plugged—'

But before Clovis could finish, he felt a kick under the table.

'Ow!' Clovis stared back at his brother. At last picking up the cue, Clovis agreed with Jahmeel, saying that there could very well indeed be a logical explanation for tonight's frightening events.

But he felt awful. He was scared and trying so hard not to show his true feelings. It was all too clear to him that an unplugged telephone could *not* work and he knew that neither Jahmeel nor himself had cut their feet earlier. The bloody footprints were real and had been made recently. But by who? Was this connected with the horrific voice he'd heard crying down the phone? Clovis had to admit to himself that there just didn't seem to be an explanation that made any sense. There only seemed to be one answer and he knew he couldn't let his mum, or his brother know. His mum would have an absolute raging fit if he told her that he'd been off investigating ghosts in an old haunted house last night. His brain desperately needed to find a scientific reason as to what had occurred in his own home.

Mum yawned and hugged her sons. She felt a little better after Jahmeel had given her a rational explanation for the phone and the footprints. Only a little better, mind, for Claudette Gayle was not a stupid woman. Her sons may not believe in the supernatural, but she did, and she could feel that something wasn't right in her own home. She decided to call Pastor Connolly in the morning. She would invite him round to do a blessing and they could have tea and some of that banana bread she'd made earlier.

Once Mum had gone back to bed, Jahmeel set to work cleaning up the bloody footprints. It had been a frightening night and even though he had tried to put a rational head on, he couldn't find a reasonable answer. He didn't want his mum to call the police because he reckoned as soon as they walked through the door they would try to accuse *him* of something. The neighbourhood was a violent one and the last thing the family needed was the locals seeing the police knocking at the front door. Tongues wagged round here, and Jahmeel was trying hard to stay out of trouble. He had to, for the sake of his mum and little brother. They needed him and relied upon him. So, calling the police and reporting bloody footprints in the house just wasn't an option.

As for the phone calls, he believed it might have been some of his mates. They were all out at a party last night and maybe they'd decided to make a late Halloween prank call. He wasn't sure how any of them had got the landline number, but he'd ask in the morning.

Jahmeel put the mop back in the cupboard and checked the floor. There was no sign of any more blood. Satisfied with his work, he made sure the front door was locked and bolted and then he made a final check on Clovis.

His brother was fast asleep, it seemed.

Slowly he clicked the door shut and went to bed.

Clovis woke up suddenly. He didn't know how long he had been sleeping, but he guessed not long.

He was aware of something heavy at the bottom of his bed. He tried to open his eyes and look but discovered he couldn't. What the hell? He tried again but struggled to prise them open. He then felt an enormous weight pressing down on his body. He attempted to cry out, but no sound escaped his lips and he realised that he couldn't open his mouth. He wanted to kick out, to scream — he needed help. What was happening to him? What about his legs? He tried to wiggle his toes and knees, but nothing. Had something fallen on him in the night? Was he *paralysed*? He tried to wrestle free, free from some invisible bond, but couldn't. What was going on? He was terrified!

Something moved on the bed. It felt like a person. Clovis held his breath. This was a real nightmare, a living one. There was no waking up from this. Then he felt heat above his face, as if someone or something were staring at him.

Suddenly to his relief, he found he could snap his eyes open. Yet, in sheer terror, he screamed as he had never screamed before.

A man's face was staring down at him. His eyes were milky white, his teeth yellow and decaying. The hair on his head was clotted with blood.

He whispered gently into Clovis's ear: 'Help me.'

CHAPTER 8

A Bullet and an Angry Apparition

The house was still and quiet, apart from the grandfather clock ticking soothingly in the hallway. It struck four and the sound of its inner workings clicked and clacked, readying itself for its hourly announcement. Four smooth chimes rang out around the ancient building, followed once more by its regular, reliable heartbeat of soft ticking.

Uncle Rufus and Eve were sound asleep. Boris lay curled up too, happy in the comfort of his master's warm bed.

The strange noise, something like the sound of someone running, woke the portly dog first. Boris lifted his head, sat up and listened. Not the quickest or most intelligent of animals, Boris certainly hadn't been acquired as a guard dog. A good job too, as he hardly ever barked unless food or excitement enticed him to. So, when the bulldog jumped off Uncle Rufus's bed and began to bark loudly, scratching at the door in a frenzy to get out, Uncle Rufus woke with a start and was instantly alarmed. Something was wrong.

Flinging on his dressing gown and slippers, he cautiously opened the door. Boris immediately sprang out onto the landing, snarling and growling like a demented monster, and ran off down the passage. Uncle Rufus turned the landing light on, only to see Boris pelting at top speed all the way back to him, a look of terror in his big eyes. The dog careered back into the bedroom and swiftly scrambled under the safe haven of the bed.

'What's going on?' mumbled Eve. She was standing outside her room, eyes half closed, her hair clumped up at odd angles, resulting from a restless sleep.

'Nothing; go back to bed.' Uncle Rufus didn't want to alarm his niece. 'I think Boris heard a cat outside. I'll go and check downstairs.' He was just about to take the first step down when he heard a noise from above. Running. Distinct footsteps.

Thump . . . thump . . . thump . . . thump. Someone was running around his attic room.

'I heard that!' Eve said, looking upwards at the ceiling.

Both Uncle Rufus and Eve stood on the landing, heads bent back, eyes wide, listening for the noise again. They weren't disappointed: *thump . . . thump . . . thump . . . thump.*

'Someone's in the house,' whispered Eve, and she moved closer to her uncle, putting her arm through his. Boris had slid out of hiding and joined them both but decided to sit on Uncle Rufus's feet for security. He whined as if in pain, his chubby folds of skin hanging down from his face as he too looked at the ceiling.

There it was again, the sound of heavy feet running back

and forth, only this time, the noise was louder and lasted longer. Boris barked. The fur on his back bristled, and drool had begun to slide from both sides of his large mouth. Eve bent down to stroke and comfort him.

'Hello, yes, police.'

Eve stood up and watched as her uncle whispered to the operator on the other end of the phone. 'We have an intruder inside our house,' he said urgently. He was just about to give the address, when the phone went dead. 'Hello . . . *hello*?' he hissed. 'Eve, try *your* phone.'

Instantly she sprang into her room, still aware of the horrendous noise upstairs, and retrieved her phone from her dressing table. She passed it to her uncle.

'Hello . . . police!' This time there was no whispering. 'Yes, can you hear me?' he shouted. He paused. 'I can't believe it,' he said to Eve. 'This one's gone dead too: battery flat. Quick, you go downstairs and use the landline, then go outside and wait for me.'

'And what are you going to do?' asked Eve, wide-eyed and very scared.

'I'm going to go up there. Now go on, off with you, go, hurry now.'

Eve turned to go, tears in her eyes.

Uncle Rufus patted her shoulder. 'It'll be all right, Eve. I'm a lot stronger than I look.'

Eve didn't respond.

Uncle Rufus grabbed an old golf club from his wardrobe,

and then as quietly as he could, he tiptoed up the stairs with Boris following closely behind him. Arriving at the top, he could see shadows moving back and forth under the door to his attic room. The sound of the footsteps was still loud but now it was accompanied by the noise of furniture being moved and dragged about.

'Right, here we go.' He looked down at his faithful companion, Boris, and took a large intake of breath. He counted to three, then turned the handle and sprang through the door with the golf club high above his head. Boris leaped forward, showing newly found courage, ready to defend his master. But there was no one to be seen. What they discovered, though, was far more disconcerting.

Eve had tried to call the police several times but just couldn't get through. The dial tone was there but after she had punched the number in, a cacophony of sound spat back at her, whirring, clicking, sputtering . . . and then nothing but silence. Realising that there must be a fault somewhere, she decided she had no choice but to go and get help from one of the neighbours. She put her coat and wellies on, while keeping an ear open for noises from upstairs, but she heard nothing. She grabbed her keys and began to unlock the heavy oak front door. She turned the handle, expecting the door to move, but weirdly that didn't happen. She pulled at it, thinking that it had become stiff with the autumnal weather, but still the door refused to budge. Eve checked that she had unlocked the door properly; confirming to herself that she had, she pulled hard again, muttering and ranting under her breath: 'What the hell! Why won't you *open*?'

She began to panic. She was trapped. But she had to get help, someone was in their house.

The back door! Eve ran through the kitchen and unlocked the little door that led into the garden. There was a gate at the bottom that opened into the back alley. If she could get to that then she could find help.

She pulled on the back door, expecting it to open immediately but nothing budged. She rattled it, tears and sweat now beginning to run down her face.

Then she heard a man's voice behind her.

'*Eve*,' the voice whispered.

She whipped round but no one was there. Although someone was now coming down the stairs.

'Uncle, is that you?'

Nothing, there was no answer. Eve was more frightened than she had ever been before.

She grabbed a frying pan hanging from a hook above her head and took a stance ready to fight . . .

. . . Uncle Rufus and Boris walked slowly into the kitchen. Rufus flicked on the light.

'Oh, Uncle!' cried Eve. She dropped the pan on the floor and ran to him.

'Oh, my dear girl! Whatever has happened? We're all right, there's no one here.'

'I heard a voice, a man's voice. He whispered my name. It was awful.' Eve began to cry once more.

'Oh, my dear, it's all right, I'm here. Nothing can harm you.' Uncle Rufus hugged Eve to him. 'You know, it could have been *my* voice that you heard. I was talking away to myself. You know how I do.'

'Mmm, maybe.' Eve wasn't so sure. The voice had sounded so clear and so *close* and it hadn't seemed like her uncle's voice. She shuddered at the memory of it.

'So, nothing upstairs?' she asked. She was regaining her composure although her face was red and blotchy, her eyes bloodshot and tired.

'I don't understand it.' Uncle Rufus looked exhausted too. 'No one there at all,' he said, more to himself than his niece. 'But the most peculiar thing has happened in the attic. All my pieces of furniture have been piled up on top of each other, and odder still is that my experiments have all been placed into a very nice neat line.'

'Has anything been taken?' she asked.

'No, nothing. I just don't understand it.'

'Surely there must have been a window left open so they could get in and out?'

'No, I checked. It's very strange. Spooky, really. I don't like it, Eve. I don't like it at all.'

'I know what you mean. Do you know, I couldn't get out

of the house. Every time I tried to pull open the door, it just wouldn't budge.'

'Really, how very strange. Let me see.' He went to the back door and pulled on the handle but again it didn't open.

'Well, this is very odd,' he said through gritted teeth. He was leaning back, using all his strength to get the door to move, but it just wasn't going to give.

'It's the same with the front door too.' Eve went to the huge door and demonstrated that indeed the door wouldn't open.

'Here, let me try,' said Uncle Rufus, pushing Eve gently to one side. He began to pull hard on the handle.

'This is ridiculous!' he shouted. Eve could tell her uncle's patience was wearing thin. She stood back and watched, feeling helpless as he yanked and pulled, trying to prise the solid oak door open, but it just didn't seem to want to.

'Come on, let's try the windows.' Uncle Rufus went into the front room and tried to push a window open, but again there was no movement. Eve raced to another one and again it didn't open. In turn Uncle Rufus and Eve tried most of the windows in the house, but with no luck. Defeated, Uncle Rufus turned slowly to Eve, looking somewhat perplexed, and, dare she think it . . . scared.

'Oh my God, Unc, do you think someone has locked us in deliberately?' Eve's voice was getting higher in pitch. She could feel herself becoming hysterical. Just the thought of someone trapping them in their own home was unthinkable.

Eve noticed her uncle had gone very pale. His eyes were huge, staring, concentrating on something. He was whispering to himself as if trying to work out a scientific problem. Eve watched him as he moved back into the kitchen.

'Right,' he said, as if coming to his senses. 'Come on, we need to go into my attic room. There might be a way that I can get a signal to the police station through one of my old radios.'

Eve couldn't believe what she was hearing. Her uncle had just invited her into his sacred place. He *must* be worried, she thought.

They made their way up the staircase once more. As they came to the first landing, Boris began to bark again. He stood stock-still, eyes forward, locked onto something on the landing.

'What is it, boy?' asked Uncle Rufus.

Suddenly something seemed to hit the landing wall. Whatever it was pinged off a picture frame and hit Eve on the side of the face.

'Arghh!' she screamed

'Oh my God, Eve, are you all right?' Uncle Rufus put his hands on either side of her face and checked her head for blood.

'What on Earth was that?' he asked.

Boris was still barking at something at the far end of the landing. But there didn't seem to be anyone there. Yet Boris seemed sure and was in a terrific state now, growling and drooling. The fur on his back was standing right up as if an electrical charge were buzzing through his stout little body.

Eve rubbed her cheek where a red mark was beginning to emerge. She knew something had hit her, but what? Getting down on her hands and knees, she began to feel around on the floor for the object that had struck her. It *had* to be there.

'What's this?' asked Eve, picking up something shiny from the floor. Holding the small object between her thumb and forefinger, she twirled it around, hoping to get a better look.

Uncle Rufus carefully took it from her and looked closely at it, turning it slowly over in his palm.

'Mmmm . . . it's a bullet.'

Eve gasped out loud. She was so confused and scared, as was Boris, who continued to snarl and bark loudly.

'Don't worry,' Uncle Rufus shouted over the noise of the bulldog's growls, 'it's been used and it's very old.' But he was astounded. Where had it come from? He had heard about this sort of phenomenon before. An apport, an object that seemingly arrives from another place or dimension. But from where, and who had thrown it?

Eve took a huge breath and tentatively took the bullet back from her uncle. She turned it about again, her face scrunched up in concentration. 'I think we would have noticed if either of us had had one of these. It's not an artefact I've ever seen lying around the house.'

'Well, I'm sure that's what hit you, put it in your pocket. Make sure you keep it safe,' he said.

'But where did it come from?'

'I don't know, and there is definitely no one here . . . Boris!' yelled Uncle Rufus. 'Be quiet!'

Boris did as his master said, but he was still not happy and began to whine softly. He sat between his two owners again, never taking his eyes off something that was clearly transfixing him.

They were just about to continue their journey up to the attic when the sound of something moving at the far end of the landing stopped them in their tracks.

A tall dark shadow was sliding slowly towards them.

Not a sound was made. Even Boris was silent. The shadow was becoming clearer. It was a man, a *huge* man. Almost as wide as he was tall.

Boris began to growl and bark again, but did not approach the strange figure. Too scared, he stayed between his master's legs.

Eve was about to make a run for it, but her uncle stopped her. He held her arm tight and whispered, 'Stay here, stay calm.'

Eve did as instructed, but clung to him for dear life. The temperature had dropped significantly and both Eve and Uncle Rufus could now see their breaths had begun to swirl around them.

It was clear that this shadow was a ghost, an apparition, a spectre.

It began to glide towards them on the landing, but it seemed to be moving in slow motion, as if it were an image caught on film but not running at the right speed.

As the apparition came closer, the footsteps were the only noise to accompany it. Its face was covered in thick red blood, which dripped down onto a white shirt. Its trousers seemed black, but no shoes could be seen.

Eve let out a scream of pure terror. Uncle Rufus hugged her to him. The ghost was practically on top of them now. Its pale white face was full of pain. It appeared to be saying something, but no words could be heard. Uncle Rufus turned around quickly, putting his back to the ghost and protecting Eve in doing so. He clung on tightly and they both held their breath.

'Help me!' The ghost's voice suddenly screamed out as if in agony, the noise was deep and desperate. Then nothing. Silence. Eve couldn't move, she dared not. The only noise she could hear now was her own breathing and the pounding of her heart.

She opened her eyes slowly, and Uncle Rufus turned his head and carefully opened one eye, nervous at what might be revealed to him. He was relieved to discover that the ghost had disappeared.

'Has it gone?' squeaked Eve.

'Yes, sweetheart.'

Eve slowly brought her head out from underneath her uncle's arm.

'Oh my God, I can't believe what just happened.' Eve was clearly shocked, as she had begun to shake.

Uncle Rufus talked calmly to his niece and tried to soothe her as best he could. Once he was assured that both she and Boris were all right, he quickly led them back down the stairs.

They went straight into the front room. Slamming the door behind them, Uncle Rufus immediately sat down and tried to compose himself. He didn't want Eve to see him ruffled. But he was jolted out of his thoughts by the crashing and banging of crockery.

'Oh, no!' yelled Eve. They both ran into the kitchen to discover smashed cups and plates all over the floor. The cupboards were open, as if someone had been riffling through them.

Just as Uncle Rufus was about to say something, more crashing and banging was heard, but this time it came from the front room. Running in, they came across the same mess. All the furniture was upside down, and books lay open, tossed about all over the floor.

Uncle Rufus went from being confused and worried to very angry. 'How dare you!' he shouted.

Eve took a step back, she had never seen her uncle lose his temper, not like this.

'Whoever you are,' he spat, 'leave us alone, we've had enough!' He brought his voice back down to a whisper, not wishing to alarm his niece any further.

It was clear he was furious and he stomped purposefully

all around the ground-floor rooms, seemingly looking for something, closely followed by Eve and Boris.

'What are you doing?' asked Eve.

'Just checking that we are alone and that the ghost has taken my advice and disappeared.' He stood dead still in the middle of the hallway, composed himself by taking a deep breath, then cocked his head to one side, presumably listening out for any strange ghostly sounds.

Eve squeezed his hand nervously, eyes scrunched tight shut, dreading any more frightening noises that she may hear.

They waited in deafening silence to see if the spirit would show itself or do anything else. After what seemed like an excrutiating age, Uncle Rufus let out a long relieved sigh. 'I think it's gone – can you feel it? The atmosphere has changed. Come on, I don't know about you, but I'm shattered. Let's get some sleep.'

Before climbing the stairs, Uncle Rufus had a last-minute thought and proceeded to try the back and front doors one last time. To his and Eve's relief and amazement, they opened with surprising ease.

'Well, whoever or whatever it was has gone now. Everything will be all right. You'll see.' Uncle Rufus smiled and hugged Eve to him.

She watched him as he locked both the doors and then one by one turned all the lights off downstairs, leaving the carnage and destruction for tomorrow. He climbed the stairs, gently pulling a very nervous Eve slowly behind him.

'I'll sleep on the camp bed in your room, so you won't be on your own, all right?' he said, yawning softly.

Eve smiled at her uncle, grateful for the fact that she wouldn't be spending the remainder of the night alone.

Boris wasn't going to be left alone either, and quickly brought up the rear. He was clearly relaxed and seemingly very relieved as he did nothing but explode loud farting noises from his rather large wobbly bottom all the way up to bed.

CHAPTER 9

An Admission of Guilt

It was now midday on Sunday and the streets of Whitechapel were deserted. The autumnal leaves tumbled aimlessly across the wet, grey pavements and puddle-soaked roads.

There was a storm brewing. The wind had begun to howl and a lone defenceless tree living in the concrete pavement whipped back and forth as if in a panicked frenzy.

Clovis and Tom stood on the steps outside Eve's house, waiting impatiently for someone to open the door. They both looked dishevelled and exhausted. As soon as his football match had finished, Tom had been the first to call his friends. He, like Clovis, was desperate to know if they had had a similarly terrifying night. The friends had briefly exchanged their frightening stories over the phone, deciding with the utmost urgency to meet and talk further. Had *they* caused this? They didn't know what was going on, and right now they needed to be together.

The front door snatched open to reveal a very tired and crumpled-looking Eve.

'Quick, get in,' she snapped. Clovis and Tom followed her

into the kitchen. Smashed plates and cups all over the floor greeted them. Eve kneeled down and began to sweep the bits of broken pottery into a dustpan.

'Wow!' said Tom.

'You should see the other room,' replied Eve. Clovis and Tom walked into the front room. It looked unrecognisable.

The treasured books that had been meticulously placed in alphabetical order were all over the place. It really was as if someone had thrown them all about in temper. The sofa had been turned upside down, as had Uncle Rufus's favourite reading chair.

Eve came into the room and ran her hands through her short spiky hair. 'I mean, just look at it!'

'Wow!' said Tom again.

Clovis was taking pictures on his phone.

'This is messed up, Eve,' said Tom.

'You're not kidding,' she said. 'And what's weirder, is this.' She pointed to the windowsill. Positioned perfectly in a neat line were some of Uncle Rufus's smaller treasured artefacts. They had been seemingly placed very carefully by an unseen hand. But whose, and why?

An old poison bottle, an Egyptian scarab beetle, a set of World War One binoculars, a Victorian crystal ball, a tiny pair of child's shoes from the Tudor period and a Roman ring.

Clovis was snapping away with his phone. 'I've heard about this. It's classic poltergeist activity. It's fascinating, although some scientists believe that this phenomenon is usually caused by a living person.'

'Are you saying that *I* did all this, Clovis?' Eve stood stock-still, her mouth remaining open in shock.

'No, no. I'm not saying that at all. It's just some people believe there is a rational explanation and it's caused by someone in the house. Someone who may be under a lot of pressure. It's called psychokinetic manifestation. Scientists still don't understand, but they believe the activity happens subconsciously when someone is under emotional stress.'

'Emotional stress!' Eve was beginning to lose *her* emotions altogether.

'Calm down, Eve,' said Tom. 'We can't all be causing these weird things to happen, Clovis. I'm sorry, mate, but in this case I don't think we're the ones responsible for anything that has happened in our homes.'

'Don't shoot the messenger. I'm just telling you what I've read. That's all.' Clovis looked back at his phone. His face was downcast. He hated it when the others didn't take his research seriously.

'Come on, guys, let's put everything back in its place,' said Tom.

Both boys took one end of the sofa each and turned it the right way up, then they did the same with the chair. One by one each item was put back on the shelves. Once everything was in its place the three friends sat down.

'You do realise that we have brought something back with us, don't you?' said Eve.

'I know it does seem that way,' said Clovis, looking defeated. He felt he had lost an argument. 'I didn't think it was possible, I still don't really, but after what I saw last night, it's made me realise that sometimes there isn't a logical explanation for everything.'

'Well, I'm telling you,' said Tom, 'I'm never sleeping in a room alone again. It was like living in a nightmare that I couldn't wake up from.'

'What are we going to do?' said Eve, exasperated. 'It's not like we can go to the police . . . "Er, excuse me, officer, but I did a Ouija board in a haunted creepy old house, contacted a dead person, and *now I have a ghost in my house*."' Her voice had gone from a whisper to shouting.

'Shush, Eve,' said Clovis. 'Calm down, we don't want your uncle to find out—'

'Find out what?'

Uncle Rufus was standing in the doorway with a face like thunder. He still had his pyjamas on but he'd put on his favourite threadbare blue cardigan and not buttoned it up correctly. He rubbed his unshaven stubbly chin and let out a huge sigh. 'I'm going to put the kettle on and make something to eat. You lot can tidy up the mess in the kitchen, then we are going to sit down, and you are going to tell me everything!'

He turned around and walked out of the room, promptly slamming the door behind him.

Everyone sat around the kitchen table, and all that could be heard was the uncomfortable sound of crunching toast. No one dared say a word. No one could look Uncle Rufus in the face. They were in trouble, they all knew it, and now it was judgement time.

Uncle Rufus sat back in his chair, cupping his hot tea in both hands. Eve watched him from under her lashes and hoped that the warmth from the mug might cheer his mood.

'Well now,' he said, his voice a whisper. All three heads hung even lower. 'It seems to me that you have got a lot of explaining to do, and from what I just overheard, it doesn't sound very good at all, does it?'

'I'm so sorry, Uncle. It was my idea. Please don't blame them. I wanted us to have some spooky fun and we thought by doing a . . .' Eve paused and looked to each of her friends for help.

'Go on,' said Uncle Rufus, his face was very stern and steely grey.

'We did a Ouija board!' blurted out Tom. 'It wasn't Eve's fault. We all decided to do it. It was supposed to be a bit of a laugh—'

Uncle Rufus put his hand up to Tom as a sign for him to stop talking.

'And where did you conduct this Ouija board?'

Again no one said a word, their eyes filled with guilt and regret. Tom could feel the sweat trickling down his back; Clovis's knee had started to jiggle up and down, a sign that he too was very nervous, and Eve? . . . Well, she just started to cry silently.

It was Clovis who spoke up first. 'We are so sorry, Professor.' He paused, looking to Tom and Eve and waiting for a sign to proceed. He would never betray their secrets without them all agreeing to it. Tom and Eve nodded, then cast their eyes down again. It felt safe there.

'We bought the Ouija board online and took a tube to Epping Forest on Halloween,' continued Clovis. 'We went to that haunted house that Eve found in some of your notes.'

Silence filled the room once more. Uncle Rufus looked at Eve and raised his eyebrows quizzically. Eve's cheeks burned. She hated the fact she had not only lied to her uncle, but she had copied some of his work without asking. Would he ever forgive her?

She feared not. Head down, eyes squeezed tightly shut, she croaked quietly, 'I'm so sorry, Uncle, I saw a rolled up piece of paper on the table and had a look at it. I saw the drawing of an old house and a map and when the notes said it was possibly haunted, well it was perfect. It was just what we were looking for. I didn't think it was so bad if I copied it and put it back. I just thought it was a project for your students.' Eve dared to look up, her uncle was staring at her in utter astonishment.

'I'm shocked, Eve,' he said in a whisper. 'I never thought you would do something like that. As it happens that document wasn't for my students, it was for something far more important. I'm at a loss, I really am and I don't know quite what to say to you.' Uncle Rufus ran his hand through his floppy fringe and rubbed his chin.

The last time something like this had happened was when she, Clovis and Tom had sneaked an abandoned fox cub into the cellar and kept it as a pet. When Uncle Rufus had discovered all his old books had been chewed, he went insane, grounding Eve for a week.

But this was worse, much worse. The three friends sat waiting for the bellowing to begin. They knew they had to take their punishment whatever it may be, but somehow they also felt relieved to be telling an adult. They were all so scared and confused about what was going on in their homes. Maybe Uncle Rufus could *help*?

But he still said nothing. Eventually he stood up, pushed his chair back and placed both hands on the table. Leaning forward, he glared at them all one by one.

Here it comes, thought Eve, shaking.

'Well now,' he began, his tone dark. 'It seems to me that you three fools have attracted something. It's attached itself to you and now Eve and I have to live with it in this house.'

'It's not just this house, Professor, it's in mine and Clovis's too.' Tom's voice was a whisper. He was too scared to speak in a normal voice in case he tipped Uncle Rufus over the edge.

'What do you mean, Tom?' he asked, leaning even further forward.

Tom and Clovis told him what had happened to them the night before.

'I'm so scared, Professor,' said Clovis. 'I've tried all the logical explanations, but it doesn't stop me from being so *frightened*.'

Uncle Rufus took a deep breath. How was he going to deal with this?

'Erm, Uncle, are you really angry with us?' whispered Eve.

'Of course I'm angry with you!' he bellowed. 'I'm angry with you all. How could you be so bloody stupid and irresponsible?'

He then ranted and shouted for what seemed like hours. He hardly came up for air. He stomped around the kitchen, walked out, slamming the door, only to come back in and start shouting all over again. Eventually though, he began to calm down and sat at the table once more.

'I'm furious with you all for lying to me and your parents and sneaking off to a forest at night on your own. What you did was downright stupid, and I hope you will never do anything like that again.'

'Are you going to tell our parents?' asked Clovis. He pushed his glasses back up to the bridge of his nose and looked pleadingly at Uncle Rufus.

'I don't know yet,' he snapped. 'But I *do* know that we have to get rid of whatever you have brought back with you.'

'We have a video,' sniffed Eve.

'A *video*! Right, let's start at the beginning, leave no detail out.'

Uncle Rufus poured himself a huge mug of tea and sat back to listen.

At that moment a huge clap of thunder rumbled over their heads and lightning lit up the house. The storm had begun.

CHAPTER 10

Into the Attic

After all their stories had been exchanged, the video was watched again. In fact, the video was viewed five times in total. Uncle Rufus's mood had lightened somewhat — actually he seemed quite rejuvenated.

He kept asking questions, all the while moving about the front room, replacing a book, moving an artefact, lastly, stoking the fire and replenishing it with coal. When either Tom, Clovis or Eve gave him an answer to one of his many questions, he began to mumble to himself as if trying to store the information. There was also a lot of 'Mmms' 'Arghhhs' and 'Oohing', which began to amuse the three friends, who still hadn't moved from the sofa.

Uncle Rufus stood still at last and turned to them. 'That footage you have captured,' he said, 'is really quite impressive. I think you have something extraordinary there. But it's pretty clear that something has definitely followed you all home.'

'But, Uncle, what can we do about it?' pleaded Eve. 'Maybe we can get a psychic or someone?'

Tom nodded in agreement. Clovis, however, rolled his eyes skywards.

'Why not, Clovis? Have you got any better ideas?' added Tom scathingly.

'I'm not doubting their abilities,' said Clovis. 'It's just there are a high percentage of frauds out there who will take money from frightened people and talk a load of rubbish. How about finding a paranormal investigator?'

'They can be just as bad too,' said Tom.

'There won't be any need for either,' said Uncle Rufus, who was brushing his pyjama bottoms down to rid himself of coal dust.

'What do you mean?' asked Eve.

She watched her uncle carefully. He was certainly behaving rather strangely. He seemed quite agitated, nervous almost.

'Come on, I feel that the time is right to share something with you. Follow me.'

Everyone did just that and followed him out of the front room and up two flights of stairs before finally they all stood behind him in front of the attic door. From his cardigan pocket, Uncle Rufus took out an ancient-looking key. He placed it into the lock and turned it once, whereupon it made a satisfying click. Then he turned the knob and pushed the door open.

Eve had never set foot inside this room before. For the last five years she had only passed meals or spoken to her uncle through a crack in the doorway. This was a monumental moment. She couldn't believe she was about to walk into her uncle's sacred place.

Tom smiled at Clovis, who looked as if he were about to faint. In fact, Tom noticed that Clovis's glasses had steamed up completely. The excitement was getting the better of him. Entering the professor's inventing room? This was a dream come true for Clovis.

Another rumble of thunder rolled above their heads and the splintering crack of a lightning bolt lit up the landing. Eve jumped and grabbed her uncle's arm. Clovis leaped and grabbed Tom's.

'For a man of science, I still don't get how you can be scared of lightning,' chuckled Tom. 'Just breathe, mate.' He nudged his friend.

Clovis gathered himself and cleaned his glasses. He put them back on, but they just steamed up again.

'Now, when we go in . . .' Uncle Rufus had turned around, his face very serious, 'I want you to promise not to touch anything, and I mean ANTHING. Do you understand?' He then stared hard at them, waiting for an answer.

'Of course, Uncle, we won't touch a thing, will we?' Eve nodded at Tom and Clovis, who in turn nodded back.

'Good, right, in we go then.' He pushed the door open wider and one by one they all stepped into a room that had been a forbidden and well-kept secret for as long as they could remember.

The space was quite large. Two big windows looked out

across the back of the garden. The wooden floor undulated, pitching and dropping, warped with time. Every conceivable space was cluttered with so much stuff. Books climbed the walls, rolled-up maps sprang out of crevices like old springs protruding from a mattress. A stuffed owl perched high on a shelf under the safety of a glass dome stared down at them with one large bulging eye. Old telescopes of every size pointed at different angles out of the windows, and there were odds and ends, wires, batteries, dummies' heads, old wireless sets, TVs and musical instruments. Glass bottles varying in different sizes and colours lined the shelves, hats ranging from top hats to tin hats hung from pegs. Huge old-fashioned clocks lined one wall, ticking and tocking at contrasting times.

As soon as they walked in, the three friends noticed the light was different in this room. It wasn't the light coming from the two windows, as it was getting darker outside with the raging storm. No, the light in this room was a soft, almost ethereal glow. Tom nudged his friends and they all looked up to see a beautiful night sky lit up on the ceiling.

'Wow!'

'Amazing, incredible!' All three were quite literally starstruck.

'It's all the constellations!' cried Clovis. He was astounded. His head was completely bent back as he turned in circles. Round and round, he went. 'Look, there's Orion and Cassiopeia . . . and there's Hydrus.' He began to laugh, pointing, spinning, shouting out weird and wonderful names.

The others smiled at his pure delight and happiness.

'This is just incredible, Professor,' said Clovis, catching his breath.

'Yes, I am rather proud of my sky. It did take me a long time to construct it. I would just get one constellation done, move onto another, and then one of the tiny bulbs would go out and so I'd have to go back to fix it. I use it to think. When I get stuck on an idea, I put my chair in the middle of the room, turn all the other lights off, and just stare up at the sky. It calms the mind, you see, and somehow it seems to inspire.'

Eventually Tom, Eve and Clovis turned their attention to the rest of the room. They stood for a while, not moving, just turning around slowly, looking at the variety of weird and wonderful objects, structures and inventions. Tom and Clovis were standing in front of a most peculiar-looking object. At first sight it reminded Tom of something a circus performer would use to entertain a crowd, but on closer inspection he soon realised this was not a toy.

An old-fashioned black bicycle hovered two feet off the floor. Two enormous red rubber balloons were tethered to either end: one to the handlebars, the other to the back mudguard. The spokes in the wheels had been transformed into what looked like tiny plastic kites and in between the handlebars a brass telescope jutted out. In front of the telescope, a small shelf was suspended by a wire. Presumably some item or other was to be placed there, so you could look at it while riding.

Eve, Tom and Clovis were transfixed. They said nothing, but walked slowly onto another peculiar sight.

A dummy's head was fashioned with what seemed to be a Mohican hairpiece. On closer inspection, they saw it was a piece of black metal that sat at the base of the skull and ran over the top, coming down into a wide visor that covered the eyes.

Again, no one said a word, not even Clovis, who was in deep thought.

'It's my Photoconductive Proton Wave device —' exclaimed the professor proudly — 'or PPW for short. I've modified the initial concept, but obviously this is a lot smaller and I can point at anything with this small camera.' A retractable cable ran from the headpiece down to the floor.

On the end, Clovis noticed a tiny camera. 'So, this camera can see right through things?' he asked, obviously impressed.

'Yes, but it also has the capability to look beyond, *behind* the subject too.' Uncle Rufus put the strange contraption on Tom's head and pressed a switch inside the visor. He then took the cable over to Eve and pointed the little camera to her shoe.

'Oh my God!' shouted Tom. 'I can see your foot. Not just your *foot*, but the bones and the floor below it!' The image was being projected straight through onto the visor.

'That's just awesome,' he said, now moving the little camera to other parts of his own body. 'Urgh!' he yelled. 'What's that? It's disgusting.'

He was pointing the camera to his head.

'That, dear boy, believe it or not, is your skull and your brain.'

'I'm surprised there's anything there at all,' sniggered Eve.

Uncle Rufus carefully took the PPW device off Tom and placed it gently back on the dummy's head.

In the centre of the room was a workstation, lights shining down onto the table. Four magnifying glasses were positioned at different angles, concentrating on something that Uncle Rufus had clearly been working on recently.

Clovis leaned in to get a better look.

A little wristwatch with its back taken off sat under the lights.

'Interesting, yes?' Uncle Rufus leaned over them.

'It's just a watch,' said Eve.

'Ah, but *is* it?' Uncle Rufus smiled then winked. 'Now then, firstly . . .' the professor stood back in the centre of the room, placing his hands on his hips and taking a deep breath. 'Before I divulge my secret work to you, I want you all to promise that you will not discuss anything you see here today with anyone. That means no pictures or videos. Nothing. Do you understand?'

Tom, Eve and Clovis all nodded their heads in agreement.

'I need you to say it out loud . . . do you promise?'

'Yes,' said Eve.

'Of course, yes,' said Tom.

'You have my word, yes,' whispered Clovis in awe.

'Right, now that's been settled, I can divulge my secret to you.' Uncle Rufus brought an old-fashioned wooden swivel stool into the centre of the room and sat down. Then he gestured for the others to sit on the floor.

'Everything you see here in my attic is an invention; a piece of equipment that I have designed and built to help capture and communicate with ... erm, how can I put this ...' He jumped off the stool and began to pace about, back and forth. He started to mumble as if having an argument with himself.

Eve was fascinated and worried. What was her uncle about to say? Did he work for the government? Was he a spy?

Seconds seemed to last for ever. Uncle Rufus was *still* pacing about and chuntering on.

It was Clovis who stopped the professor in his tracks.

'Ghosts!' he exclaimed. 'All these inventions are to capture and talk to *ghosts*, aren't they?'

Uncle Rufus stopped dead in his tracks and stared straight at Clovis. 'Yes,' he said. 'That's right, my boy. That's right.'

CHAPTER 11

Up, Up and Away

'What! No way! That can't be true, can it, Uncle?' Eve stood up and stepped towards the man who had looked after her all these years. The man who took his work at the university so seriously. He had won awards, been asked to give talks on quantum physics. Why would he be spending his time, *all* his spare time, inventing ghost machines?

'Clovis is right,' said Uncle Rufus. He spoke quietly, almost embarrassed to look Eve in the eye. He took her hands in his. 'All these objects and inventions are to try to communicate with the dead.'

Clovis looked very pleased with himself. Tom nudged him and smiled.

'How come?' said Eve, 'I mean, I don't understand. You've never even talked about ghosts or anything remotely connected to them. The only thing that I've ever seen connected with ghosts is the drawing and notes of the haunted house that I found.' She looked at her hands, and guilt washed over her face once more. Taking a breath, she continued: intrigue had taken over. 'But that was just a history research project, wasn't it? There aren't any books on the subject in your library, well, none that I've ever seen. In fact, if anyone ever told a creepy ghost story, you were the first to question it. Or call it an urban myth. So why do all this?' She gestured about the room.

Her face fell. She looked so hurt, so wounded, that her only relation could keep such a huge secret from her.

Uncle Rufus smiled lovingly at her. 'I think I need to explain myself. Let me tell you why. I think you will understand after you've heard my story.' He took a big intake of breath. 'Do you remember yesterday when I told you, Eve, that I thought I'd dreamt about seeing your aunt? Well, it wasn't a dream, it was real, *she* was real, and she came to me one night in this house.'

He proceeded to tell them the most incredible tale. How he had woken up one night to hear the crockery being moved about in the kitchen, the cupboards being opened and closed. Thinking the obvious, that some intruder had broken into the house, he had grabbed his trusty golf club and slipped quietly down the stairs.

'I was expecting to see a burglar and was prepared to knock the scoundrel out. When I got to the bottom of the stairs, I could feel an icy blast of cold air, the hairs on the back of my neck were standing up like poles. Then I saw Boris, just sitting there, looking at something or *someone*. His tail was wagging, and he seemed quite at ease. I called out, but I didn't get a reply. And as I walked into the kitchen . . . there she was, making a cup of tea! My Jess! I couldn't believe my eyes. I actually pinched myself to see if I was dreaming. Of course I wasn't, but seeing Jess so clearly, going about our kitchen as if she had never left, quite literally took my breath away. When I called her name, she turned around and looked as solid as you or me. She was beautiful, like an angel, her skin was like porcelain and her eyes shone like blue crystals. I tried to touch her, but my hand went straight through her body. Then she smiled and slowly disappeared. I don't mind admitting it to you all, I cried like a baby. Then as I wiped my face, I felt a gentle kiss on my cheek and heard a voice in my ear. It was so soft, like a baby's breath.'

Uncle Rufus went quiet and glanced down at his feet.

Eve put her hands over his, and asked, 'What did she say, Uncle?'

Uncle Rufus smiled at his niece. 'She said, "I'm always with you." '

Tom and Clovis gaped at each other.

'Until then, I'd never believed in ghosts or life beyond this one. I'm a scientist through and through. But when I saw my wife, my beautiful wife in our kitchen, standing there so solid and real, my whole world, everything I'd ever believed in, was blown out of the water. I was desperate, you see. I needed, *wanted*, to see her again.'

'And so, by making all these inventions, you hope to see and talk to her again?' asked Eve.

'Exactly, my dear. If I could just take her in my arms once more . . .' Tears filled the professor's eyes. Eve hugged her uncle tight, understanding completely why he had dedicated all his time to this cause. It made perfect sense now.

'Does any of it work?' asked Clovis. 'I mean, have you actually been able to speak to ghosts?'

'Well that's a very interesting question,' said the professor. 'And the answer is that yes, a lot of it *does* work, and I have been able to speak to ghosts, but never the one I most want to speak to — my beloved Jess.'

No one was sure how to reply to that. It was so desperately sad that he hadn't been able to achieve what he wanted, but also so incredibly exciting that he'd actually been able to communicate with the dead.

'This here,' continued Uncle Rufus, patting the seat of the bicycle and balloon contraption proudly, 'is my first ever invention that worked. It needs a few tweaks here and there, but it mostly does the job.'

'What *does* it do exactly?' asked Tom.

'Well, I think the best thing is for someone to ride it, and then you will get the idea.' Uncle Rufus had the biggest grin on his face, and of course Clovis with his long legs was able to stretch up and be the first to straddle the bike.

'Now, Clovis, when you pedal, and you must pedal quickly —' instructed Uncle Rufus — 'the wheels will spin in a different way to the way you're used to. As such, they create an energy that changes the atmosphere around them, one metre in radius, to be precise, and when you are at full speed, any item you put in front of the telescope will dematerialise.'

'*This* I've got to see,' said Tom, shaking his head in disbelief.

Uncle Rufus took a pencil out of his cardigan top pocket. 'See here, I'll place this pencil in front of the telescope, and when Clovis pedals and creates a new enclosed atmosphere, you'll see that the pencil will –' Uncle Rufus clapped his hands together once – 'disappear, just like that.'

'Go on then, Clovis, start pedalling,' urged Tom.

'Now, you two, come over here and look at this small monitor. It's connected to the telescope, so we can see exactly what's going on while Clovis pedals like the clappers.'

Clovis began to pedal. It took a while to get up to speed, but once he did, the wheels began to rotate quickly, whirring round with a strange whooshing and clacking noise. Tiny white sparks began to fly out of the machine, but they didn't disappear, they began to swirl around the whole bike like a cyclone. The faster Clovis pedalled, the louder the noise became, and the cyclone of bright white sparks began to whip around Clovis and the bike at a whirlwind pace. Slowly but surely, much to the amazement of Tom and Eve, the black bicycle began to rise further into the air.

Uncle Rufus quickly undid the tethers that held it down and threw his arms up in the air. 'Off you go! Ha, ha! Isn't it marvellous!'

Higher and higher, the bike lifted up. Poor Clovis gave a high-pitched shriek. 'Oooooooooooh!' Clovis was looking down at his friends, not quite believing what was happening to him. Instantly, in the shock of being lifted off the ground, he stopped pedalling and wobbled in the saddle. 'Woahh! What's happening, Professor?'

'Keep pedalling, Clovis, don't worry. Pedal like mad,' shouted Uncle Rufus.

Tom and Eve shouted encouraging instructions to their friend, his legs going round and round, his glasses all steamed-up and with a look of fear etched on his face. Eventually it was just too funny for Tom to hold it together any longer and he burst out laughing. A squeaking, farting noise brought Clovis's head up to the ceiling as the balloons rubbed the rafters of the attic. He was floating at the top of the house!

Tom, Eve and Uncle Rufus looked on at the spectacle: Clovis was riding a bike on nothing but thin air.

'Wow!' shouted Eve.

'Oh my God, that's insane!' said Tom, having managed to compose himself.

The noise of the wheels had become loud and the little kites on them had caused a wind that was whipping round the room.

All of a sudden, Clovis let out another high-pitched scream.

'What's happening?' shouted Eve.

'Are you all right?' asked Uncle Rufus, concerned.

'It's OK, I just feel a bit funny,' shouted back Clovis.

'That will be the change in the atmosphere around you. Keep pedalling, you're nearly there,' encouraged Uncle Rufus. 'Now watch the pencil closely,' he commanded. Tom and Eve huddled around the monitor and stared at the pencil on the screen.

It was held into position by a little clip. Nothing out of the ordinary seemed to be happening . . . until one end of the pencil began to disappear. Then slowly a bit more faded, until eventually the whole thing had vanished.

'Look, there. It's gone!' Uncle Rufus pointed, and he began to laugh in excitement.

Tom and Eve just stared, mouths open. They looked at each other, then back at the monitor. They were speechless.

Clovis was still pedalling as if he were desperately trying to get away from something. The wheels of the bike couldn't be seen any more, but they could be heard. The telescope bumped and bounced around.

'Look through the telescope, Clovis!' shouted Uncle Rufus.

Clovis lifted his steamed-up glasses onto his head and placed an eye to the telescope. 'It's gone!' he exclaimed. 'How is that even possible?'

'Once you start to slow down, the pencil will materialise.' Uncle Rufus was really enjoying himself.

A huge fork of lightning lit up the room and thunder rumbled angrily above the house, but no one blinked an eye at the storm outside, they were all too amazed to see their friend hovering above their heads on a bike.

'Oh wow! That is just amazing!' cried Clovis. He had stopped pedalling now, and slowly the bike had begun to descend back down to the floor. Once again, he looked through the telescope and exclaimed, 'It's back! The pencil, it's back.'

Eve, Tom and Uncle Rufus couldn't tell if he was panting from excitement or all the manic exercise he had just done.

Uncle Rufus went on to explain how the balloon bike helped in the hunting of ghosts. 'If I can make something solid disappear, then surely, I can make it *reappear*. A ghost is made of different kinds of atoms and I'm working to change the atmosphere so I can capture and materialise a spirit. I know it sounds very odd, but I believe this will be possible in time. It needs a lot more work, but I think I'm on the right track.'

After Eve and Tom had both had their go on the balloon bike, Uncle Rufus showed them his communication board. It was a small wooden panel filled with letters, words, pictures and numbers, and behind each character was a lightbulb.

'This can be used when there is knocking phenomenon. I still haven't got to the bottom of this sound yet, but strange knocking noises seem to come from the floors and walls in most haunting cases. I've found that this occurs just before an entity appears, either fully or sometimes vocally.' Uncle Rufus turned the little board on.

It reminded Tom of an electronic game he once had when he was little.

'What exactly *is* this knocking they do?' asked Eve, about to touch one of the letters, but quickly pulling her hand back when she remembered her uncle's warning.

'I believe ghosts use it as a way to communicate with us. I think they are talking to us, and because they exist on a much higher plane, with a higher vibration to us, we can't hear them normally. But when their words are slowed down, we hear them as knocks.'

'Like the sound barrier?' added Clovis.

'Yes, exactly, so when a plane hits the sound barrier it makes a *BOOM* noise. I think we are dealing with something similar. It's a very crude theory but hopefully these inventions will prove there is something to it. So, this little board can be very useful. For example, when you hear knocking, you can point to a letter, word or number and the ghost will knock to let you know which character they have chosen. For instance, if I'm talking to a spirit and I ask, "How are you feeling today?" I would then point at these words.'

Clovis, Eve and Tom bent over the board, their heads all close.

'So,' said Tom, 'there's *naughty, happy, sad, excited, lonely, angry.*'

'Yes, so, I point to each word and when they knock, I then know how they are feeling.'

'It's like a Ouija board, then, but without a glass?' concluded Clovis, running his fingers over the words, but careful not to actually touch the board.

'I've discovered the knocking phenomenon isn't new, people have been reporting it for centuries. It always seems to happen in famous hauntings. It really does intrigue me, and this machine has proven very useful so far in dozens of cases.'

'You've spoken to ghosts with it, then?' asked Tom.

'Yes, one or two.'

'You just said "dozens of cases".'

'Well, yes, that's the thing. A few people have borrowed my inventions over the years.'

'Really? Who?'

'I'm afraid I'm not at liberty to say. I just hope *we* can put this machine to the test soon.'

Eve, Tom and Clovis looked at Uncle Rufus, all of them picking up on the word '*we*'.

'This is all so amazing!' Clovis's excitement could no longer be contained. He hugged the professor, much to both their surprise.

'Oh, my goodness, my dear boy.' Uncle Rufus was smiling from ear to ear. 'I'm so pleased you like it. I thought you wouldn't care for these kinds of inventions, as I know you don't believe in ghosts.'

'I didn't, but just recently they've really interested me. And after what happened last night – well, I do believe in *something.* I just want to use science to find out what it is, and your pioneering creations are just the best.'

Eve moved around the room, looking at more strange objects and weird paraphernalia. There was an old camera connected to a radio, their cables entwined like spewed-out spaghetti. In one corner stood an object that really caught her eye. She had no clue what it was, but it looked fantastic.

It was an old copper bath with four small wheels attached underneath. In the middle sat a tall black box. Crystals of every shape and colour were inlaid on each of the four sides. Then the crowning glory: four enormous gramophone horns stuck out at different angles. In between the big horns sat what looked like smaller ones, but on closer inspection they appeared to have once been trumpets. The little horns protruded out, gleaming and shiny ready to produce a note or two. On either side of the crystallised black box, large copper antennae jutted out at odd angles.

Clovis and Tom noticed that inside the bottom of the bath, water was present. Tom got onto his back and slid underneath it to take a closer look at the underside.

'There's heating filaments under here,' came his muffled voice.

Uncle Rufus began to smile.

'What does it do, Uncle Rufus?' asked Eve.

'Well, it took me for ever to invent it. I shall put you all out of your misery. My dears, gather round. Let me introduce you to Messenger One.'

Eve, Tom and Clovis just stared.

'But what exactly does it *do*?' repeated Eve, walking around the odd-looking machine.

'It's something to do with talking, right?' asked Clovis.

'Exactly right! I've discovered through my research that it's possible to have conversations with ghosts.'

'That sounds creepy,' said Tom, his voice echoing back as he had pushed his face into one of the horns.

'So how does it work?' asked Eve.

'Well, once plugged in, the filament under the bath warms the water which in turn heats up the crystals,' said Uncle Rufus enthusiastically, walking round the machine and explaining the science behind his invention. 'The antenna picks up on the purest radio waves that we, or any known living creature, cannot hear. We talk through this mouthpiece which then converts to radio waves which shoot out into our atmosphere and then they, the dead, talk back to us. The crystals help to transfer the pitch, modulation and tone of their replies into voices which we can hear loud and clear through these horns.'

'Wow! That's amazing,' said Clovis 'But can I ask . . .' he paused, looking a little embarrassed. 'These pieces of equipment look pretty old-fashioned. You don't seem to be using any modern technology?'

'A good observation, Clovis. I discovered that the Victorians seem to have had more phenomena and communication with the deceased than we do with all our modern gadgets. So, I think going back to basics is the key.' Uncle Rufus smiled and patted one of the horns on Messenger One. 'But if you look here, you will see a USB port. This is where, I don't mind saying so myself, I struck upon a genius idea.' He trotted over to his workstation and picked up the old wristwatch he'd been working on. Placing it into the palm of his hand, he presented it to Tom, Eve and Clovis.

'This little watch isn't just for keeping time, it also records audio, or EVP.'

Eve and Tom looked confused.

'Electronic voice phenomena,' said Clovis confidently.

'Exactly,' said Uncle Rufus.

'What's that?' asked Tom.

'It's when a ghost talks, but you don't hear its voice with your ears.'

'Is that because they are on a higher frequency?' asked Eve, looking pleased with herself.

'Correct. I'm impressed, Eve, you *were* listening. This watch can be worn all the time. It's recording our frequency and theirs. You wouldn't be able to hear their voices played back normally but you *can* when it's plugged in and played through Messenger One.'

'That's amazing!' said Clovis.

'Can I put it on?' asked Eve, staring at the little watch.

'Not yet, but I promise you will be the first to try it. If that is what you'd like?'

'So, does that mean we can use this equipment to find out who's haunting us?' asked Tom.

'Well, yes, that's exactly what I'm hoping, but I'm not sure your parents would be very pleased with me if you started using my machines. If we're successful, you might have nightmares.'

'I think it's too late for that,' said Tom.

'Come on, let's go downstairs and have something to eat.' Uncle Rufus opened the door of the attic, only to find Boris lying across the floor. He opened an eye, let out an explosive fart, licked his chops and went back to sleep.

CHAPTER 12

Contact is Made

Everyone made their way towards the kitchen. They were all talking excitedly at once about the machines and the likelihood of them working, asking Uncle Rufus when they could give them a test run, arguing playfully about who would be the first to capture a ghost. But their chatter was brought to an abrupt halt when they entered the kitchen.

Everyone froze to the spot. A stomach-churning fear gurgled up through Eve's body. Tom stumbled backwards, nearly taking Clovis and Uncle Rufus down with him.

All the chairs from every room in the house had been placed in a perfect pyramid structure on top of the kitchen table. The small kitchen chairs sat at the bottom, on top of them straddled the front room dining chairs, and above *them*, at the pinnacle, an inch from the ceiling, sat Uncle Rufus's favourite reading chair. The cupboard doors and all the drawers were open too.

'Arghh!' shouted Tom.

'Noooo!' screamed Eve.

'Wow!' said Clovis.

'Oh my!' said Uncle Rufus, walking around the room, looking carefully at the perfectly balanced chairs. 'I'd forgotten about our ghostly visitor for a moment or two.'

'Oh my God, this is crazy. I feel sick,' said Eve, grabbing Tom's hand. It was a frightening spectacle to behold. For something to cause objects of this size to move on their own and to be placed in such a precise order was very creepy and beyond belief, but here they all were witnessing it.

'It's incredible!' cried Clovis, taking pictures on his phone.

'Right,' said Uncle Rufus. 'There's no time like the present. Whoever this ghost is, he's determined to get our attention, and I think we can definitely say he's done that. Eve, go back into my attic, please, and bring down the communication board. Perhaps we can try to talk with our visitor.'

While Eve ran up the stairs to retrieve the board, the others began to take the chairs down from their precarious positions. Once the table was cleared and the kitchen chairs were back in their rightful place, Uncle Rufus positioned the boys around the table. When Eve arrived back with the board, he placed the communication device in the centre of the table and everyone sat quietly, waiting for Uncle Rufus to begin.

He turned the little machine on and they all watched as the board lit up in readiness to receive its first message.

'Now let's see if our ghost wants to come and talk to us,' whispered Uncle Rufus, rubbing his hands together excitedly.

He took a deep breath, closed his eyes and began to talk out loud.

'Hello! We know you're here; we know you are watching us. You've wanted our attention, well, now you've got it. Tell us who you are.'

Everyone looked at each other, wide-eyed and a little fearful.

Suddenly the table began to shake.

'Can you feel that?' whispered Uncle Rufus.

'Oh my God! Yes,' squealed Eve. She was clearly excited.

Tom stared, mouth open in astonishment at the movement of the table.

'Extraordinary,' said Clovis, pushing his glasses back up the bridge of his nose.

The table began to bang about now; it jumped back and forth with a life of its own. Then they all began to hear knocking noises, as if someone were tapping underneath the table.

'Ah, it's here,' said Uncle Rufus, smiling with satisfaction.

The board lit up like a Christmas tree. Everyone gasped. Now for the test. Would the knocking be able to activate the words and letters on the board?

'I will point to the letters and you, my dear friend, must tap on a letter to make your words. So, let's begin.'

Uncle Rufus slowly pointed to the letters, and sure enough the ghost began to light up the board, illuminating certain ones.

T.A.L.K.   T.O.   J.A.N.E.

Then the computerised voice spoke: 'Talk to Jane.'

Uncle Rufus sat back in his chair, looking aghast.

'Uncle? Are you all right?' asked Eve, concerned. 'You don't look good.'

'Yes, sorry, it's just I think I know who this Jane is.' He leaned forward closer to the board and whispered a question: 'Is your name Finlay?'

Two explosive knocks jolted the table up in the air.

'What does that mean?' asked Tom, a little shaken.

'Two knocks for yes, one for no,' replied Clovis, looking very pleased with himself.

'So, you know this ghost?' asked Eve, clearly puzzled.

'Yes, I know who this person is or rather *was*,' replied Uncle Rufus. He shook his head in amazement and asked another question. 'Finlay, what do you want us to do?'

They all sat waiting for the board to light up or the table to bounce about, but nothing happened.

'Has he gone?' whispered Tom, looking about him nervously.

Uncle Rufus asked the question a few more times but silence was the only response.

'I think he's gone for now,' he said.

'Who are Jane and Finlay?' asked Eve, getting impatient now.

Uncle Rufus stood up and began to pace the room, the colour in his face had returned.

'Jane Bains is Finlay's daughter. She's an old university

lecturer of mine. We became firm friends and have always kept in touch throughout the years. She was very good to me when we lost our family in the accident. Well, just recently she visited me at the university, because I'd told her about my inventions over the years and lately she'd been the recipient of a lot of strange paranormal phenomena and haunting dreams. She believed her late father Finlay needed help. She said his ghost had appeared to her several times and she kept dreaming of him in a house in the middle of the woods. She was obviously upset by all of this and wanted my help. She gave me some information about a house in Epping Forest which she felt was significant to the case. Information *you* came across.'

Eve looked at her feet, embarrassed.

'Ahhh, so *she's* the person who gave you the stuff about the cottage,' said Tom.

'Yes, and I was doing some research and planning to visit, but you beat me to it.'

'Oh, Uncle, we *are* sorry,' said Eve.

'Well what's done is done,' he replied. 'It certainly seems Jane was right, though.'

'Should we not call this Jane and tell her what's just happened? That's what the ghost – I mean Finlay – wanted, didn't he?' Clovis looked to his friends for confirmation.

Everyone agreed.

'We can do better than that. We will all go to see her. Come on, everyone, grab your coats. We're off to Hampton Court.'

CHAPTER 13

Jane Bains

They all squeezed into Uncle Rufus's faithful little Mini. It was a very old, bright red car and had a number plate that read *SC13 NCE*. Slowly but surely, they made their way out of Whitechapel and onto the A3.

An hour later, the little classic car was bumbling through the streets into Hampton Court. The palace that was once a home to Henry the Eighth loomed magnificently in front of them as they came into the village. Eve, Tom and Clovis had never been to this part of London before, and oohed and ahhed at the palace, the boats on the river and the horses in the fields.

Eventually they slowed down as they drove up a narrow lane. Uncle Rufus pulled up outside a quaint little cottage. Before the engine had been turned off, an old lady was already opening the door.

'Rufus!' she exclaimed. 'How wonderful, and who are your young friends? Come, come inside, all of you. There's a fire going, and I've just put the kettle on. It's so chilly, isn't it? Good drive?'

The woman was small in stature and had a welcoming manner. Her hair was white and tied in a bun that stood to attention on the top of her head. Eve liked her immediately.

'Jane! Lovely to see you again.' Uncle Rufus sped up the little path and nearly knocked the old lady down. 'I'm sorry to drop in like this, but we just *had* to see you.'

'Of course, of course. Come inside, all of you, or we'll freeze out here.' Jane motioned to them all with her walking stick.

They were shown into the front room and Uncle Rufus introduced Jane to everyone properly. The fire was crackling in the hearth and a big plump sofa waited to be sat in. Eve, Clovis and Tom did just that. Clovis narrowly missed being punctured in the buttocks by a vicious pair of knitting needles.

Jane bustled out of the room and returned a few minutes later with a tray laden with cups and saucers, a large teapot and a selection of cakes.

'Here, let me take that,' said Clovis, jumping up to help.

'Thank you, young man,' said Jane, and she slowly lowered herself into a large armchair.

Meanwhile Tom was looking about the room and noticed lots of photographs in frames sitting on the mantelpiece and all over sideboard. Black and white faces of old family members, he presumed, next to modern photos of babies and weddings.

Eve was more intrigued by a white sheet that was covering

something. It sounded as if some sort of animal were underneath it. She thought it was a cage that had been covered up. The size and shape gave it away. She could hear something fluttering inside it.

Then to everyone's surprise there came a high-pitched squawk.

'Hello! Hello!' the strange voice shouted out.

'Oh, please forgive Mister Pig. He gets very excited when guests come calling,' said Jane, giggling.

'I'm guessing that Mister Pig is a bird?' said Clovis, as he poured tea into the cups.

'I will introduce you,' said Jane. 'Tom, be a dear and take the sheet off the cage. Slowly, mind, Mister Pig doesn't like fast movements. He's forty years old now. We've grown old together, he and I.' She sat back and closed her eyes briefly as if in pain.

Tom slid the sheet off the cage slowly and carefully, so as not to scare the animal, and sat back to admire the most beautiful parrot.

'Wow!' said Eve. 'He's gorgeous.' She kneeled down in front of the cage and peered at the bird. His beautiful plumage was a shimmering green, with fiery red feathers on the sides of his wings, and his small beak was yellowy orange.

'He's awesome,' cooed Tom.

'You can open the cage if you like. Mister Pig will join us and he may talk if he so wishes. He has a mind of his own. Any rude words he says, I take no responsibility for. That's why he has his name. His old master was a sea captain who loved to swear. Disgraceful! Mister Pig loves company and has the run of the house. I've tried many times over the years to let him loose in the garden but he just stays by my side and has done for all these years.'

She leaned forward and began to pass the cake around. 'Help yourselves, but watch your fingers, Mister Pig is rather partial to a bit.'

The cage door was opened and after a while the bird climbed out and flew the short distance to Jane's armchair, where he perched for the remainder of the visit.

Uncle Rufus finished his tea and popped the last of the cake into his mouth, wiped away the crumbs and then stood up.

Mister Pig squawked in alarm: 'Pooh on a stick!' The bird's words were loud and certainly a surprise. He fluttered his brightly coloured wings at the sudden movement of Uncle Rufus, stared sideways at him from his beady eye and then squawked, 'Arse!'

Tom, Eve and Clovis screamed with laughter.

'See what I mean?' said Jane, her face burning with embarrassment. 'Filthy, naughty boy!' she scolded. The bird cocked its head and bobbed up and down on Jane's shoulder. 'Cake! Cake!' he demanded. Jane sighed, and placed a tiny crumb in the bird's beak. He enjoyed it thoroughly, closed his eyes and seemingly went to sleep.

Uncle Rufus cleared his throat. 'So, Jane, the reason for our visit is that I have some information about your father.'

Jane put down the teacup she was holding. 'Really? You've been to the house I told you about?' she asked.

'I haven't, no. But the kids have,' said Uncle Rufus. 'And it seems you were right. Your father's ghost was at the house, and what's more, he seems to have followed Tom, Eve and Clovis home.'

'Followed you home?' gasped Jane. 'How is that possible? How do you know?'

'Let's just say he's been trying to get our attention,' replied Uncle Rufus. 'But we've actually managed to communicate with him today, using some of my inventions. And it seems he wants help.'

'Help?' gasped Jane. 'What with, for heaven's sake?'

'That's what we don't know, Jane. So, we thought we'd come and speak to you and try to get some more information.'

Jane leaned forward in her chair and picked up her teacup again.

'Well I'm not sure where to start, really. My father, Finlay, was apparently an extraordinary man, although I was only six years old when he was reported missing in action. I have very few memories of him, but I'm told he spoke several languages, was an eminent mathematician and historian, and that he was highly prized by the government. He was a very busy man, but when he was home I do remember him teaching me to swim one summer and reading me *Alice in Wonderland* night after night before bed. When he disappeared, my mother was devastated and never quite got over it.' She stood up slowly and took the black and white picture of a man in uniform down from the mantelpiece, tracing his face with her bony finger. 'It was nineteen-forty, and Britain was in the grip of World War Two. My father was the best at what he did. He was an agent for Special Operations Executive.'

'What's that?' asked Eve.

'He was a soldier who went undercover, did the most extraordinary things to try to destroy the enemy from within. He was sent away on very dangerous missions. My mother never really knew what he was doing, but she knew that one day he might never return. It was her biggest fear. He was only young when he disappeared. At the time, his commander told my mother that he was on a mission that had gone wrong and he never reported back to headquarters.'

Jane passed the framed picture to Eve and the boys. Instantly Eve and Clovis gasped out loud. They recognised him. It was the ghost that they had both seen but, in the photograph he wasn't covered in blood, he was handsome and young, with dark hair swept over to one side and medals hanging from his uniform. He didn't look frightening now.

'Why do you think he's haunting us?' asked Eve.

'I had a heart operation a few months ago,' continued Jane, 'and during that operation I died on the table for a few seconds apparently. And I saw this beautiful white light coming towards me and then . . . I saw him.'

Clovis was entranced. 'Saw who?' he asked.

'My father Finlay. He looked exactly as you see him in

that picture. And he walked towards me, holding out his arms. We embraced and I felt nothing but love. It was beautiful. He told me that it wasn't my time and I had to go back to the earthly plane, because he needed my help. He told me that he had to "escape from the house".

'So, when I got out of hospital, I decided that I must try to discover what happened to my father and what "the house" might be that he was talking about. My mother had been given very little information and our questions had mostly fallen on deaf ears. She had told me that his disappearance had something to do with Epping Forest, but that seemed strange, as most of his missions were abroad. Well, I had an old colleague at the university who was an historian and I had him delve into my father's file. So much of that information was secret during and following the war, but now it was more freely available. He tracked my father's last mission to being in Epping Forest — so that much was true indeed — and to a group of Nazis he was infiltrating. His mission was to find a secret underground Nazi war room and destroy it. The house I told you about, Rufus, was mentioned.'

Eve looked over at her uncle and felt a flash of shame that she'd spied on his private matters.

'But the Nazis never invaded mainland Britain,' pointed out Clovis.

'A good point, young man. But it seems a few might have got behind enemy lines and secretly built an operations headquarters — maybe in Epping Forest. Of course, my friend found the house, but said there was no evidence whatsoever of a Nazi war room there.'

'Have you been to the house in Epping Forest yourself?' asked Tom.

'Not yet,' replied Jane. 'It's a long way for me to get to at my age and on my own. I was hoping to go soon with Rufus. When my friend could find no sign of my father, I decided to get in touch with your uncle, who I knew was making incredible advancements in the world of the paranormal. When I told him all about the story, he was fascinated, weren't you, Rufus? And keen to come with me, once he'd done a little research of his own and finalised an invention he was working on.'

'And I would have done if this lot hadn't got there first.'

'Yes, I'm sorry,' said Eve. 'I found your notes and decided the cottage would be a good place to experiment with a Ouija board.'

'Oh dear, that's very dangerous,' said Jane.

'Yes, we know that now,' said Tom. 'But at the time we thought it would be fun.'

All of a sudden Mister Pig squawked loudly: 'Finlay's here, Finlay's here!'

'Oh, and that's another thing; Mister Pig can't stop talking about my father. I think he can *see* him,' said Jane proudly.

Tom looked about nervously, not wanting another onslaught of paranormal activity. Not just yet. He wasn't sure if he was ready.

'Ever since that vision of my father when I was on the operating table,' Jane said urgently, 'there seems to have been a window of communication left open between us. I think I know why he is haunting you, he needs your help. Unbeknown to you, you must have opened a channel into his world and now we are the only ones that can help him. He wants you to continue, I think, he wants you to find his body.' She was becoming breathless now.

'Quick, Tom, get Jane some water,' ordered Uncle Rufus.

'He was a good man, my father, you must help him. You must find him so he can rest and be at peace. He's in limbo, I think. Neither in this world or the next. Please help him.'

'Hush, Jane,' said Uncle Rufus, offering her the water. 'Have a rest. Please don't overexert yourself.'

Jane sank back into her chair and closed her eyes. Within minutes she appeared to be asleep. Mister Pig fluttered his wings and began to clean his feathers with his beautiful beak, never leaving her side.

'Is she all right, Uncle?' asked Eve concerned.

'She's fine. I think it's too much excitement for her. She's nearly ninety, you know. She's tough but I fear time is against us, we must get back to the house and plan.'

It was half an hour before Jane woke up. Uncle Rufus made her some more tea and once he was satisfied that she was well again, they said their goodbyes.

'I will call you, Jane, when we have something to report,' said Uncle Rufus. 'You mustn't worry yourself. We will help your father, I promise you.'

Everyone piled into the car and waved goodbye as they drove off up the lane. Jane waved enthusiastically with Mister Pig happily perched on her shoulder.

On the way home they all talked at once, high-pitched voices chatting excitedly.

'I can't believe the Germans actually got into this country!' cried Clovis.

'Now . . .' interrupted Uncle Rufus. 'I don't need to tell you that everything we have learned today is to be kept secret. This is something that must not get out to anyone. Do you understand?' He twisted the driving mirror so he could look at Tom and Clovis scrunched up together in the back seat of the tiny car.

They both nodded in unison. Just by looking at the professor's eyes, they could tell he meant business.

'This is a secret that none of us will utter to anyone,' said Eve. She took her uncle's hand and held it tightly. 'I promise.'

Uncle Rufus smiled, squeezed her hand back, then let go as he crunched the gears and accelerated up a small hill.

CHAPTER 14

A Plan and a Grateful Ghost

Amongst much excited chatter, an impressive dinner was made. Tom, Eve and Clovis helped Uncle Rufus, peel, chop and mash. As they ate at the kitchen table, they discussed Jane's father and listened to each other's theories as to what could have happened to him.

'I think we all agree that we have to help Finlay,' said Uncle Rufus. 'By doing that, we will also help Jane. All her life she has wondered what happened to her father. Well, now hopefully we can find his body and then Finlay can finally rest.'

'And I think Jane will too,' said Eve.

'Yeah, she didn't seem very well. Do you think she's hanging on to life until we help her dad?' asked Tom.

'It's sad to say but yes, Tom, I think you might be right.' Uncle Rufus wiped his mouth with a napkin and pushed his finished plate away from him. 'Our ghostly visitor has already followed you all home, much to the anguish of your parents and your brother, Clovis. I think for the meantime, until we have solved this mystery, it's only right that you both stay here with Eve and me. I really don't think your parents would enjoy another night of paranormal antics, do you? I will give them a call.'

'But what will you tell them?' asked Tom, looking worried. 'It's not as if you can say —' he dropped his voice and put on a posh accent — '"I hope you don't mind but Tom's staying here with us tonight because he has a ghost following him about!"'

Everyone chuckled: his impression of Uncle Rufus was rather good. Yet even though he had made everyone laugh, Tom was nervous. He knew his dad could be difficult and he didn't want the professor to have any bother.

'Don't worry, I'll tell them that you are both helping me with some university research. Which isn't a lie. If we can help Finlay, then I can write a paper on the subject for the university, and Tom . . . my voice isn't *that* posh . . . is it?' Uncle Rufus smiled at Tom, who nodded that it was.

'This is great, I'll feel so much better if we're all together tonight,' added Eve. Relief ran through her. She had been secretly worrying about the night ahead and didn't want another repeat of unexplained ghostly behaviour.

'Right, well that's settled then,' said Uncle Rufus, clapping his hands. 'I'll make the calls; you lot tidy up the kitchen.'

Clovis's mum, Claudette, was happy for her son to be partaking in such important university work, but she did ask that he eat a proper meal and didn't go to bed late.

Tom's dad, Dan, grunted his approval down the telephone

line and then hurriedly rang off as apparently the big match was about to start on the TV.

Then after all the dishes had been washed and put away, Uncle Rufus instructed Clovis and Tom to cycle home, pack a bag for the week, not to dawdle and come straight back.

The boys did just that and returned within an hour. Nothing had followed them home, which was a relief for everyone.

They all sat in the front room, the fire crackled casting orange shadows that danced about the room.

'What about school?' asked Tom. 'Finlay might follow us there.'

'I think we should try to go,' said Clovis. 'I think our parents would be really upset, especially my mum, if she found out that I hadn't been. And if none of us show up, I think that would look really suspicious.'

'I agree,' said Uncle Rufus. 'See how it goes tomorrow and if our ghostly friend does try anything at school then I'll think of something.'

'Also,' added Eve, 'we could use the school library to do a little research. You know, on all things paranormal.'

'Good idea,' said Uncle Rufus. 'Look up famous hauntings and ghosts. Try to look for any patterns in their behaviour. It's all very fascinating and will help you and your confidence enormously.'

He bent down to stroke Boris, who lay dozing at his feet. Boris lifted his head, snorted in contentment and then promptly let out a deathly ripple of a fart.

'Boris! You really are a smelly dog,' said Tom, holding his nose.

'So, what do we know about our ghostly friend?' asked Uncle Rufus. He sat forward, pulling from his top pocket a pen and a small, tattered old notebook.

'Well, he's very angry,' said Eve, hugging her knees for comfort.

'We think he was murdered by the Nazis,' said Clovis.

'Yes, I think you might be right there,' said Uncle Rufus, jotting down the points made.

'When Eve and I saw him on the landing he had blood dripping down his head and face.'

'And that may match the bloody footprints that we found in our flat,' said Clovis.

'What else?' asked Uncle Rufus. He tapped the end of his pen onto his teeth, deep in concentration.

'What about the bullet that was thrown at you?' asked Tom, nudging Eve.

'Yes, that's a good point.' Uncle Rufus was writing quickly. He stood up and took an old magnifying glass from a shelf.

'Have you still got the bullet, Eve?'

Eve took the metal object out of her pocket and handed it to her uncle. He carefully placed it on the table and began to inspect it under the magnifying glass.

'Mmm, it's definitely World War Two, it's from a pistol. Here you can see on the bottom its serial number: L18A1 RG 06.'

'What do those numbers mean?' asked Eve, squinting her eyes to look at the tiny numbers.

'They identify what kind of ammunition it is. How large it is and where it's from,' replied Clovis.

'Is there anything you don't know?' smiled Tom, rather proud of his friend.

'We can check the serial number tomorrow at school,' said Eve. 'Also, when we did the Ouija board in the house, it spelled out "*B.E.L.O.W.*" when we asked where the ghost was.'

'Do you think that means he's in a cellar or somewhere below the house, or was he talking about Hell or something?' asked Tom.

'Let's start with the cellar idea,' said Uncle Rufus.

'So, are we definitely saying that we have contacted a ghost called Finlay and that he followed us home and is now haunting us because he needs help?' whispered Tom. He looked about, feeling uncomfortable, aware that this ghost could be listening to everything they were saying.

'Yes, it seems to me,' said Uncle Rufus, 'that Finlay desperately needs our help.' He stood up and walked over to the fireplace. Rocking gently back and forth on his heels, he warmed his hands behind him. Then he turned to face the fire. 'We need to go back,' he said.

'Go back where?' asked Tom.

'To the haunted house.' Uncle Rufus turned around to find all three friends staring wildly at him as if he had lost his mind.

'Are you joking, Uncle?' asked Eve, standing up.

'Why would I joke about something like that? I'm serious. But this time, I will come and so will Boris, and we'll take some of my equipment.'

There was a long pause, the only sounds that could be heard were Boris's snoring and the fire that spat and crackled.

'I think he's right, it makes sense to me,' said Clovis.

'When were you thinking we should go back?' asked Tom, nervously biting his thumb.

'Tomorrow night, the sooner the better,' said Uncle Rufus. His eyes sparkled in the firelight. Tom, Eve and Clovis couldn't help but smile, his excitement was infectious. 'I've also been thinking about school. I think you should take Tuesday and Wednesday off.'

Tom punched the air and shouted 'Get in!' as if he'd just scored a goal for England.

'Tomorrow night could be a late one,' continued Uncle Rufus. 'You'll need the next couple of days to recover. I will speak to your parents and the school.'

That night they all bunked together in the front room. No one wanted to be alone just in case Finlay decided to pay a ghostly visit. The fire had died down and the last embers glowed red, making light shadows flicker over the sleeping faces. Boris's snores came regularly, rolling like a barrel lurching over rough terrain.

The night passed quietly; nothing stirred — not a bump nor a ghostly bang.

When morning came everyone began to get ready for the day ahead. Uncle Rufus's voice cut through the happy banter between the friends as they eagerly got dressed.

'Quick, everyone, in here!' he shouted from the kitchen.

Eve, Tom and Clovis charged in to find a most peculiar and eerie sight. The table had been covered in white flour.

'Look!' instructed Uncle Rufus, pointing to the centre of the table. At first no one could see what he was pointing at, but as they all neared closer to the table, they could see that someone or something had written in the white flour with big, bold letters: *THANK YOU.*

'That's bizarre,' whispered Eve.

'And creepy,' added Tom.

'Wow!' exclaimed Clovis, snapping away on his phone.

'To think an entity from an alternate plane has been able to write and leave us a message!' said Uncle Rufus. He was also taking pictures and then he began to jot down notes on his little pad. 'This is incredible, really quite something,' he continued. 'There are historic famous cases where ghostly writings, footprints and handprints have been discovered. I was always a little dubious but now it seems that it's *really* possible. I assume Finlay has heard our plan and is grateful. Wonderful! What a morning!' Everyone talked at once, pointing at certain letters, walking round and round the table, taking pictures.

'Do you think Finlay has stopped being disruptive because he knows we are going to help him?' asked Eve.

'I imagine so,' said Uncle Rufus. 'You were probably the first people he could communicate with in years. Finlay used that opportunity to find help and we now know that's what he was after all this time.'

'So do you think he was murdered in that house?' asked Tom.

At that moment the table began to shake, as did the chairs. The flour plumed into the air, falling everywhere like fine snow.

'Woah!' cried Tom.

'What the . . .' gasped Eve, grabbing hold of her uncle.

Just as quickly as the shaking started, it stopped.

'I think that could possibly have been a heavy truck going past the house,' said Clovis, walking towards the window to get a better view of the street.

'No, there was none, and our house wouldn't shake like that even if a bomb went off. I'm afraid even though I admire your logical thinking, our ghostly friend was replying to Tom's question,' said Uncle Rufus.

'What?' gasped Tom, his mouth open wide in amazement.

'Go on, ask again, ask if he was murdered?' encouraged Eve.

'OK,' replied Tom nervously. This time he held onto a chair to stop it from tumbling over. 'Erm, hello.' As Tom spoke, he chewed on his thumb and looked up to the ceiling, imagining a ghost staring down at him from above.

'Keep going, Tom,' reassured Uncle Rufus.

'Were you murdered? Shake the table if you were.'

Straight away the table began to shake, but this time so violently that the legs underneath began to make a cracking sound as if at any moment they would snap off.

'Wow! OK, thank you,' shouted Eve seemingly at no one.

'That's so scary, he can hear us,' whispered Tom.

'We got your message, thank you,' said Uncle Rufus. 'I can assure you we will all do our best to help you and your daughter Jane. But can I ask you not to cause any more chaos in my home? It *is* getting a tad tiresome. And also, may I ask if you would kindly remain here with me? The kids need to go to school and I don't think they need any more distractions.'

The table began to shake again and ended with a loud bang, almost as if the ghost had used his fist to knock under it.

'I'll take that as a sign that you agree,' smiled Uncle Rufus. 'Right, chaps,' he continued. 'Off to school with you all, and remember not a word to anyone about our visitor or our plans. Be back home as quickly as you can and then we'll make our way to Epping Forest.'

Eve, Tom and Clovis began to grab their belongings. No one uttered a word, everyone in shock as to what they had just witnessed. But they all agreed as they rode their bikes towards school that they couldn't wait to get back home and begin their adventure.

CHAPTER 15

Back to the Haunted House

Eve, Tom and Clovis attended their lessons but in truth they just couldn't concentrate. Their minds were elsewhere, thinking about the evening to come. They were going back to the haunted house. A place that truly terrified them all — but they had decided together that they had to do it, to help this ghost.

They all felt better knowing that tonight Uncle Rufus would be with them. But if any of their school mates found out what they were up to they'd think they had gone crazy. It was imperative that they keep their secret. They must never tell a soul about where they were going and what they were about to do.

They all met up in the library at lunchtime and descended upon the one free computer.

They searched for information on paranormal activity, and in one hour they had watched footage of seances, Ouija board sessions, EVP recordings and famous pictures of ghosts caught on camera.

They whispered and nudged each other, being careful not

to attract any attention. The last thing they needed was for a teacher to ask what they were doing.

Just before the bell went at the end of lunchtime, Clovis asked Eve to get out the bullet that had been thrown at her.

He searched online for ammunition that had been used during the war. He looked at dozens of images of bullets that looked similar to Eve's, and wondered what importance the bullet had for Finlay.

Why launch it through the air at Eve?

'This *must* be a clue,' said Tom, moving the cursor across the screen.

Images of bullets in different shapes and sizes flooded the computer.

'Look at that one, it's worth hundreds!' pointed out Tom. 'Shame he didn't throw that one at you, eh?' He nudged Eve playfully but she didn't respond.

Her eyes had locked on to the picture of a little copper bullet, its design and stamp matching hers perfectly. 'That's it!' she shrieked.

'*Shush*,' whispered Clovis, looking about him. 'Let's see.' He clicked on the image to enlarge it and sure enough it matched.

'It says it's for a Luger 9mm pistol. It was used during World War One and Two. It's a German pistol!'

'Wow!' said Eve. She blew out a long breath then rolled the bullet across her palm. 'So, it's true then, the Germans *were* here.'

Just then the bell rang and everyone in the library began to pack up their books and move to their next lesson.

'Do you think the bullet is the one that murdered Finlay?' whispered Eve, as they walked slowly down the corridor.

'I would think so. I mean why else would he throw it at you?'

'Well, we can ask that question tonight when we go to the house,' said Clovis under his breath.

'I can't believe we are going back there again,' shuddered Eve.

'Me neither,' said Tom.

The remainder of the afternoon went by quickly and it wasn't long before Eve, Tom and Clovis were pedalling furiously through the streets to get back home.

Walking through the door, they nearly tripped over four rucksacks in the hall that were piled high, bulging at the seams.

'Ah ha! Fabulous, perfect timing,' said Uncle Rufus, smiling. His hair was standing at odd angles and he'd obviously had a very busy day. He looked as if he were about to go and climb Mount Everest. He was dressed warmly, and on his feet he had a pair of sturdy walking boots. 'I've made us some sandwiches and hot chocolate to have in the car on the way. Can you all get changed quickly, then grab a rucksack. Eve, you take Boris, I'll lock up, and I'll meet you at the car.'

Without saying a word, Eve, Tom and Clovis did just that.

Boris was straining at the leash with excitement. It was as if he knew he was going on an adventure and he couldn't wait to get started. His stubby tail moved back and forth, which in turn pushed his chubby rotund bottom left and right. If he became any more excited, he could quite possibly fall over or just explode. Jumping up and down, which was a great feat for the little dog, Eve led him to the car, which he promptly tried to get into. But being so portly, he couldn't quite manage it. Tom bent down and lifted Boris's bum up and began to push him in and at that precise moment, Boris decided to let out a rip-roaring fart right into poor Tom's face.

Tom was not happy.

Eve and Clovis doubled over with laughter; tears streaming down Eve's face.

'It just means he loves you,' she said, wiping the tears away.

'I love him too, but that was disgusting,' said Tom.

Everyone piled into the car; Eve in the front and Tom, Boris and Clovis in the back. The rucksacks were pushed between everyone, so it was a very cosy fit. Uncle Rufus pulled out of the estate and they made their way through the rush hour traffic.

To pass the time they ate their sandwiches and drank the delicious hot chocolate. Eve told her uncle about the information they had found on the bullet. They discussed what possible connection it could have to the ghost, then talked about famous hauntings. It wasn't long before they had come out of the city and were travelling on the quieter roads. The light was beginning to fade as they reached the perimeter of the forest. Eve instructed her uncle which road to take. He drove slowly, turning the windscreen wipers on as a soft drizzle began to fall. The trees loomed down on them as they moved at a snail's pace along the quiet dark forest roads. The daylight had completely gone now, and the Mini's headlights guided them to where Eve thought the haunted house lay.

'I'm sure it's around here,' she said, looking closely at all the trees and bushes. Suddenly she recognised the area and the clumps of bushes they had walked through.

'There!' she cried confidently, pointing to a thicket of bushes that looked as if they had been parted in the middle.

Uncle Rufus pulled up the little car and turned the engine off.

'It's just through there,' said Eve, thrilled that she had managed to remember the spot.

'I can't believe we're about to go in there again,' whispered Tom.

'Me neither,' said Clovis, who looked like he was about to go into battle. Torches, temperature guns, microphones and even a stethoscope all protruded from a black utility jacket that he had put on over the top of his coat. Clovis had prepared himself — which hadn't surprised his friends at all.

'OK, before we go in, I just want to check we have everything we need.' Uncle Rufus's eyes glistened with excitement in the dimly lit car. Everyone got out and walked to the front of the vehicle. The professor took his rucksack and tipped the contents onto the bonnet.

'Now, in each of your bags I have packed the following . . .' He held the items up one at a time. 'One torch, one walkie talkie, one electromagnetic field meter or EMF for short, and one GoPro camera, which you can clip onto your coats.'

'Wow! These are cool and so tiny,' said Tom, picking the small camera up and looking at the tiny lens.

'I've modified them so they will record in night vision. And . . .' Uncle Rufus rummaged around inside his bag and produced a small, steel tin which he opened up slowly.

Eve, Clovis and Tom huddled around, intrigued as to what surprise he was about to spring on them.

Inside the metal tin, sitting snugly in black sponge foam, lay four identical watches.

'We all have one of these,' he said. 'I've been working on them for a while. The one you saw in my attic was the last one.' He took out each watch, one at a time. 'If you look on the back, you'll see I've inscribed them with your names, so you don't get them mixed up.'

Everyone turned the watches over and looked closely at the back. On each one an intricate design had been engraved into the silver. The symbol of a snake swirled around itself in a figure of eight. Its mouth was open wide, devouring its own tail. Their names had been written inside one circle and the words *Venator Exspiravit* in the other.

'What does that Ven-a-tor . . . Ex-spir-a-vit mean?' asked Eve, spelling the syllables out one by one. She had never come across such strange words before. She ran her finger over the shiny silver letters as if stroking some delicate tiny animal.

'It means *ghost hunter* in Latin,' replied Clovis.

'And the snake?' asked Tom.

'It's an ancient symbol that means life everlasting,' added Clovis, smiling smugly.

'I'm impressed, Clovis. There is a little more to it than that, but that's a story for another day,' said Uncle Rufus, smiling. 'Right now,' he went on, clapping his hands together, 'we need to strap these watches on and get going. Are you all happy?'

'Happy? I'm ecstatic! I can't believe it,' cried Eve. 'These are amazing.'

'Our own EVP recorders. Unbelievable, Professor.' Clovis was holding the watch as if it were made of glass.

'It won't break,' laughed Uncle Rufus, strapping his own one on.

'Thank you so much, Professor, this is fantastic. I shall look after it always,' said Tom, clearly delighted at such an unexpected and unusual gift. And he gave Uncle Rufus a hug.

Uncle Rufus was quite taken aback. He coughed and spluttered his thanks, then quickly brought the conversation back to the matter in hand.

'In my bag I have the communication board.' Uncle Rufus

patted it affectionately, as if patting Boris. 'Let's hope it gives us lots of information tonight. This little beauty has never let me down yet, and I have to say, I'm really rather thrilled with it.' Uncle Rufus smiled warmly at the machine.

'I'm almost too scared to touch it,' whispered Eve.

'And so you should be.' He laughed and began carefully to put all the equipment back into his rucksack. Then he and Clovis, deep in some kind of scientific conversation that neither Tom nor Eve could begin to understand, began walking slowly towards the house, with Boris snuffling along closely behind them. The other two hung back.

'Are we ready to do this?' asked Eve.

'No, but we've got to, haven't we?' said Tom, biting his thumb.

'Yes, we have,' replied Eve, smiling. 'C'mon, it will be all right. Uncle Rufus is with us this time. We'll be fine.'

CHAPTER 16

A Secret Revealed

Boris was the first to go into the house. He ran in quickly, barking and snarling as he went. Something was in there, and Boris was determined to find it. The others followed behind, their torchlight bounced off trees and bushes, causing huge black shadows of themselves to wrap around the front of the disintegrating building.

Eve watched her breath swirling about her, and realised her heart was pounding through her chest. Last time they had been here they had been petrified beyond belief and now here they were back again. Were they crazy? She shook her head, remembering why they were doing this. Jane and Finlay needed their help. She felt her confidence rushing back as she pushed the old wooden door further open.

It creaked loudly as it begrudgingly gave way to let the returning visitors in. Old bits of wood and crumbling bricks lay scattered about on the floor, the smell of damp leaves and moisture filled the thick dank air. The ghost hunters walked carefully into the first room on the right, scanning the decaying grey walls and dirty floors. It looked exactly as they remembered it, even the old newspaper was still there.

Everyone scoured the derelict rooms for a door down to a cellar. It *had* to be here somewhere, but no door could be found. Coming back into the front room, Eve noticed Boris behaving oddly.

The little bulldog was sitting in the middle of the room, staring into the corner. His tiny curled-up tail wagged back and forth, his big head cocked to one side as if he were listening to someone talk.

'What is it, Boris?' said Eve, walking over to him. She got down on her knees and looked to where Boris was so transfixed. 'I can't see anything,' she said. 'There's nothing there, Boris.'

'Don't be too sure,' replied her uncle. 'As we've both witnessed, young Boris here is excellent at detecting if there is a spirit with us.'

'Is it Finlay?' wondered Tom, looking about him nervously.

'Well there's only one way to find out. Shall we set up the communication board?' asked Clovis, clearly keen to get things going.

'Excellent idea,' said Uncle Rufus, beginning to clear a space for them all to sit down.

Tom moved closer to Clovis and the others. He, like Eve, suddenly felt rather frightened and had begun to regret stepping back inside this horrible place. There really was something awful about the atmosphere.

'Are you all right, Tom?' asked Uncle Rufus.

'Yeah, sorry, just a bit nervous,' he replied, turning about and pointing his torch in every possible direction.

'It's OK, Tom.' Uncle Rufus placed a hand on his shoulder. 'If you prefer you can always go back to the car,' he said gently.

'No way!' Tom replied. 'I'm not missing this. I might be a bit nervous, but I want to see what happens.'

'Good.' Uncle Rufus smiled in the torchlight and went back to his space on the floor. He opened his rucksack and brought out the communication board, which he laid carefully in front of them.

'Put the EMF meters all around us in a circle. That way we'll see and hear if something is close by. Once a ghost comes close to the machines, their energy interferes with the electromagnetic field. The lights will flash and there will be a static noise that emits from the boxes.'

Clovis, Tom and Eve placed the little boxes about them in a circle just as Uncle Rufus had instructed. Boris was still intrigued by something in the darkest corner of the room. Whatever or whoever it was, obviously wasn't causing Boris too much concern; he seemed more inquisitive than frightened.

Uncle Rufus then turned the board on. It lit up and made a short ringing tone, alerting everyone that it was ready to begin.

'Right, Eve, do you want to start? Call out for someone to talk to us.' Uncle Rufus nodded to his niece to begin.

Eve cleared her throat. She looked over at her two best friends and smiled nervously.

'Hello, is there anybody there?' Her voice was small and shaky. As if in answer, a small breeze whistled in from outside, sending a chill around the dark room.

'Go on, ask again,' said Clovis, looking over his shoulder nervously.

'Hello.' Eve's voice was louder and more commanding this time. 'Is there anybody here with us who would like to talk?'

Straight away the EMF meters all began to squawk loudly, buzzing and squealing. The different coloured lights on top of the boxes skipped and flashed brightly. Something had interfered with the atmosphere. Something was closing in on them.

Tom's voice whispered in the eerie dancing light. 'I feel as if someone's walking around us, you know, like, checking us out.'

'Yeah me too,' agreed Clovis.

Suddenly a knocking noise seemed to be coming from under the floor. It was very quiet at first, soft thuds which quickly grew into loud knocks.

'Who are you?' asked Clovis. His face was a picture. Eyes wide, brow furrowed, mouth open in deep concentration, he stared hard at the board. Silence filled the room, no one moved a muscle. Everyone's heads were bent down and they all stared at the board and listened out for a knock. Suddenly it came, loud and clear, one letter lit up.

F was the first character to be illuminated, accompanied by the bizarre computer voice. The letters kept coming and eventually the voice spelled out the name 'Finlay'.

'Hello, Finlay!' whispered Uncle Rufus. Everyone huddled closer together.

'Can you ask him to confirm that he died here?' asked Tom but Rufus didn't have a chance to direct the question to the board as it was already answering.

'*K.I.L.L.E.D   H.E.R.E   M.U.R.D.E.R.E.D.*' The computerised voice vocalised the letters one by one, then when the ghost had finished what he wanted to say, the words were spoken out together, forming a sentence. It all sounded very strange and creepy as the deadpan electronic voice echoed around the dark eerie house. The sound was deafening and truly terrifying.

No one spoke, the only sound that could be heard was the rain now pelting down outside. Again, a breeze blew in and made the room colder, if that was at all possible. Eve shook, she didn't know if it was from fear or from the drop in temperature.

'Finlay?' whispered Eve. 'Where is your body?' She knew what the answer would be.

Sure enough, the computerised voice spelled out the word: '*B.E.L.O.W.*'

'Do you want us to find your body, Finlay?' asked Uncle Rufus.

Again, another loud silence filled the icy room. Eve had

scrunched her eyes shut, as had Tom. Clovis was still staring hard and Uncle Rufus waited hopefully.

The knocking began again, the lights flashed, and the voice simply said '*Y.E.S.*'

'Can you tell us how to get down there?' asked Eve.

'We've been all over what's left of the house—' Tom was interrupted by the voice of the computer spelling out more letters.

'*F.I.R.E.P.L.A.C.E.*'

'What!' exclaimed Eve, standing up in excitement. She darted towards the fireplace and began to feel around it. 'Do you think the fireplace is a secret doorway?'

Uncle Rufus put the communication board back in his bag and joined Eve.

'It could very well be.' He pointed his torch up inside the black chimney. An unexpected explosion of frenzied activity barraged out of the dark chasm. Multiple black-winged creatures flew out, emitting high-pitched screeching noises. The black shadows encircled everyone, diving and swooping and releasing a moment of mayhem.

Eve screamed, dropping her torch; it rolled about on the floor, causing the light to bounce around and creating more confusion. Tom squealed and Clovis screamed like a small child as he grabbed hold of Tom for security.

'It's all right, everyone,' cried Uncle Rufus. 'I've just disturbed some bats. They won't harm you.' He began to chuckle, sticking his head back up the chimney. 'And I think if I just pull . . .' His voice became muffled. He sounded as if he were struggling with something. 'Aha!' he cried, and then the noise of a metal object being pulled could be heard. Suddenly his head popped back out of the fireplace and something extraordinary happened. Slowly the whole wall and front of the fireplace began to move and swing open like a door, to reveal what looked like an old rusty cage.

'Hey presto!' shouted Uncle Rufus, a massive grin spread over his face.

The cage was just a bit taller than Uncle Rufus and large enough to accommodate about four people. Its door was a metal gate that slid to one side to let people in and out.

'It's an old elevator! Wow, this is incredible!' exclaimed Clovis. He leaned in and began to examine the structure.

'I don't like this at all,' said Eve. She was really worried now. This ghost hunt had started out as a simple, innocent adventure, but with each day that passed it was turning into a living nightmare — and now this! An elevator, leading to where? Eve wasn't happy, wasn't happy at all. She stood back from the rest of the group, not sure what to do.

'Right, listen carefully,' said Uncle Rufus. 'This is up to you now. I totally understand if you don't want to carry on, but if we don't, I think Finlay may well continue his hauntings until he finds peace.'

'Can't we tell the police?' asked Eve.

'Not yet,' replied her uncle. 'We need some evidence.

And right now, no disrespect to Finlay, no one would believe us.'

'But we've been recording everything on our cameras and watches, surely we can take those to the police as evidence. And so far, Finlay has been right,' said Clovis, pointing wildly at the newly discovered elevator.

'Yes, we could, but we don't know how good the recordings are yet, and as for the EVP on the watches, we won't know what the quality will be like until we get home and plug them into Messenger One. The police will need more than just a dream that an old lady had about her dad. We need to get as much evidence as possible. Trust me, when I've passed on paranormal evidence to the police in the past, they are not the easiest people to convince. They need one hundred per cent proof before they can get involved.' It was clear now that Uncle Rufus had been investigating haunting cases for quite some time, but just how involved he was with the police, the others had no idea.

It was obvious that he was determined to carry on. 'If you like, I can continue on my own. I totally understand if you don't want to come. It's very scary. And if Finlay is right – as you've pointed out Clovis, he hasn't been wrong so far – who knows what horrors may lie ahead. This job isn't for the faint-hearted.'

'Job?' asked Eve.

'I meant what we're doing here tonight.' Uncle Rufus shifted from one foot to the other. He looked down to his shoes as though something fascinating had caught his eye on the floor.

'I don't know,' mumbled Tom, unsure.

'Well, I'm with the professor,' said Clovis. 'How often do you get to have an adventure like this?'

Moments slipped by. The wind was getting stronger now, and it howled outside like an enraged animal while the rain pelted hard against the cracked grimy windows. Drops of water began to plop down from the ceiling into the room.

Eve went to her uncle; taking his hand, she whispered, 'I'm in.'

'So am I,' said Tom. 'Although we must be nuts,' he added, smiling and shaking his head in amazement.

'So, do you think this goes down to the Nazi war room?' asked Clovis, peering inside nervously.

'I have no idea, but shall we see if it works?' Uncle Rufus said excitedly. He grabbed the handle and with great difficulty tried to slide the metal cage open. 'It's very rusty, come on everyone, let's pull it together.'

Eve, Clovis and Tom scrambled forward and took a hold of the metal gate. After much huffing and puffing and teeth clenching, the stubborn old gate gave way. Eventually Uncle Rufus stepped cautiously inside. He shone the torch all around the little elevator to get a closer look. Two large white buttons sat next to each other on one side, on each of them a letter was written, one with the letter *B* and on the other, *G*. A mirror ran the whole length of the back of the elevator, obviously intended to make the small compartment seem much larger to passengers, and to top it off, a tiny chandelier hung down in the centre of the ceiling. It once would have been beautiful, now it drooped down, wilted, dirty and covered in cobwebs and dust.

Uncle Rufus walked in and began to jump up and down on the spot.

Eve gasped in shock. 'Uncle, no!'

'Don't worry, Eve, I'm just testing to see if it's secure.' A mischievous smile spread across his lips. 'Shall we take a ride and see where it goes?'

Boris needed no time to think about it; he shot inside and sat between his master's legs. His tongue dangled, panting with excitement.

Eve, Clovis and Tom looked to each other. No one said a thing. Surprisingly it was Eve who walked in next, followed by Tom, then lastly Clovis squeezed in.

'Slide the gate closed, dear boy,' commanded Uncle Rufus.

Then Eve held her finger above the button that had a B on it. She looked to her uncle, who nodded. She pressed the button and closed her eyes.

Nothing happened. Everyone looked at each other nervously.

'Well, I'm not surprised really, it needs electricity to work,' said Clovis, who was squashed in tightly between Tom, a rucksack and Eve. His glasses were now steamed up and crushed across his face. The elevator was clearly made for two people to travel comfortably, not four and a flatulent dog.

Just as he said that, an electrical buzz resounded around them, and the dusty little chandelier flickered on and off. Then, without warning, and to everyone's shock, the old elevator plunged straight down.

CHAPTER 17

A Ghostly Guard

After the initial stomach churning descent the old elevator thankfully slowed down. It began to rattle and moan like an angered beast waking from a long, deep sleep. Where they were going was a complete mystery. No one spoke, uncertainty and fear etched on their faces. The little crystal chandelier bounced about above their heads, projecting a dirty, dim orange glow and strange blinking lights over the frightened faces.

The journey seemed to go on for ever, falling down further and further into seemingly nowhere. After about a minute the elevator came to a sudden and dramatic stop. Everyone stood completely still, no one daring to move or speak. The only noise that could be heard was the tinkling of the chandelier. Its little teardrop crystals banged about, clashing into each other as if surprised at such unexpected movement. Then finally, one long, loud sound of electricity buzzed about them, shutting off their light source.

Uncle Rufus clicked his torch on and directed the beam upwards, bringing a welcome bright light into the small enclosed space.

'Everyone all right?' he asked.

'Just about,' breathed Eve. It was in fact the first time she had taken a breath since she had walked into the elevator.

'I'm OK,' whispered Tom, nibbling on his thumb.

'Me too,' added Clovis. 'What I don't get is that there didn't seem to be any electricity in the house ... so how come the elevator works? It must have another source.'

'I think you're right there, the electricity supply must come from down here,' said Uncle Rufus, pointing the torch out of the front of the elevator.

'Where is *here*? Where *are* we?' whispered Eve.

'That's a very good question, my dear girl, and I think we are about to find out ... Here, hold my torch, Tom.' Uncle Rufus grabbed the handle of the elevator, pulled hard, and slid the metal cage door open. Taking back his torch, he walked slowly out of the enclosed space. The others followed, huddled together for security. Everyone clicked their torches on, bringing their new surroundings into light.

Cobwebs lit up like silver beads as the beams of light slid over them. They seemed to have arrived in someone's front room. It was small and compact, with a metal door on the opposite side. They could make out furniture and pictures on the walls, though of what, they couldn't tell, as everything was covered in thick dust. An overturned armchair, a smashed cup and saucer on a round table. A small wooden bed lay in the corner of the room, its blanket still crumpled as if someone had only just woken up.

'Looks like someone left in a hurry,' said Clovis, peering closely at the objects around him.

'Look at this,' whispered Eve. She was standing over an old black wireless set that sat on a side table in the corner of the room.

Uncle Rufus came over to inspect Eve's find. 'It's a German wireless and it's very rare, from the nineteen-thirties. In fact . . . this whole room looks like it's been stopped in time.' He went over to a big picture that hung over the mantelpiece. He wiped the glass quickly with his sleeve and found the dust came away easily. The face he uncovered took everyone's breath away. There in the dark, staring straight at them, was a face that represented nothing but pure evil. It was the cruel and furious gaze of the dictator Adolf Hitler himself.

'Oh my God!' said Eve, stepping backwards. 'They really made it, the Nazis actually got into this country.'

'If Mr Mason could see this, he'd have a heart attack,' said Clovis.

'Well, your history teacher can never know. Remember, everyone, not a word.' Uncle Rufus's voice was serious and stern.

He moved around the small room, dusting down more pictures. Faces of German soldiers appeared on the walls one after the other, their silent smiles looking down on them all.

Tom had discovered an old newspaper on the floor. It was the London *Herald*. The black, bold headlines read *BATTLE OF BRITAIN RAGES ACROSS SOUTHERN SKIES*.

'Look, this paper is dated nineteen-forty, so that ties in with when Finlay went missing.' Tom folded the paper up carefully and put it in his rucksack.

Boris growled suddenly. The noise was menacing and scary. He started to walk backwards, his eyes fixed on something in the corner of the room.

'Uh oh,' said Eve, knowing that when Boris barked or growled, something spooky was imminent.

Suddenly the old wireless lit up like a small beacon, emitting a red glow around the small room. Then came the voice. A horrendous noise that no one would ever forget: a distinct man's voice, shouting and growling in German. The hideous noise hissed and spat through the damp air. Louder and louder it went, sending shivers all over Eve's body. Everyone stood still, stone-cold with fear. She snapped first, and screamed: 'Turn it off!'

Uncle Rufus rushed to the radio and tried to do just that. He pressed every dial and button but nothing happened. He kneeled down to find the plug but there wasn't one. Boris began barking continuously, his hackles up like little spikes.

The voice boomed loudly about them all. Eve and Tom had their hands over their ears. Remembering the similar incident with his own TV, Tom realised that if left alone the device would soon turn off.

'It will stop on its own, Professor!' he shouted.

Sure enough, the radio clicked off moments later. The voice disappeared and the eerie red light began to fade.

Everyone breathed out, except Boris, who was still looking in the opposite corner of the room.

'Get your EMF meters out,' instructed Uncle Rufus. 'Someone is with us, and I don't think it's Finlay.'

Tom, Clovis and Eve brought out their little machines and passed them to the professor, who then laid them neatly on the floor close to the corner of the room where Boris was currently standing guard.

Straight away the meters began to screech with electricity, the lights on the top all flashing, letting everyone know that something was present that was not of this world. Boris stopped barking and sat down, but his eyes never moved from the corner.

'It's gone very cold all of a sudden,' said Clovis, pointing a temperature gun into the corner. 'In fact, in this part it's minus four degrees but in the middle of the room it's . . . fourteen degrees!'

'Really? That's very interesting, Clovis,' replied Uncle Rufus. He took a deep breath and began moving towards the corner of the room. 'Who are you? Who's there?' he asked, never taking his eyes off the dark, cold space in front of him.

'Be careful, Uncle.' Eve's voice trembled, still shocked from the radio.

'Did you hear that?' asked Tom, looking about him nervously.

'Hear what?' answered Clovis.

Tom stood absolutely still, as if frozen in time. 'There it is again, you sure you can't hear that?'

'What *is* it, Tom?' asked Eve, feeling really anxious.

'*Shush*, everyone . . . I can hear it too,' whispered Uncle Rufus. 'It's a man's voice, he's saying one word over and over again. It's here. It's not coming from the radio, it's coming from this corner.' Uncle Rufus was stood facing the dark space, his hands outstretched to feel the drop in temperature. All of a sudden, his body doubled over as if someone had punched him in the stomach. He yelled out in pain and then to everyone's horror they watched as his body lifted off the floor and fell backwards through the air.

'Arghh!' Yelling in pain, he landed on the ground with a thump.

Then a deep voice boomed around them clear and deep, so loud that everyone heard it this time. 'NINE!' Eve screamed and placed her hands over her ears.

Tom and Clovis rushed to Uncle Rufus's side and helped him up.

'Are you all right, Professor?' Tom asked.

'Yes, I'm fine. I felt as if someone thumped me and then pushed me out of the way. Extraordinary, really, quite extraordinary! Fascinating!' Uncle Rufus brushed himself down and went over to Eve, who by now was crying.

'My darling girl, are you all right? I'm fine, there's no need to cry,' he said, hugging her.

'Oh, Uncle, it was so awful seeing you being hurt like that!' Eve slid down the wall and sat with her knees bent and placed her head in her hands.

'I can cope with anything, Uncle, but I don't want you to be harmed.'

'I'm fine, my dear. Look!' Uncle Rufus began to do a little dance on the spot to prove that he was indeed unharmed.

Eve began to laugh and immediately felt better.

'Did you all hear that voice?' she asked.

Tom and Clovis nodded in stunned silence.

'Nine?' said Tom.

'I think it was "Nein",' said Uncle Rufus. 'It's German for "no". How extraordinary. I do love hearing vocal phenomena. I wonder why it shouted that?' Uncle Rufus looked deep in thought.

'I think whatever was here with us has gone now. Look, Boris is half asleep,' said Tom. He went over to the dog and stroked his now very relaxed body.

'Tom's right,' said Clovis. 'Look, the EMF machines have all stopped too.' He began to collect all the devices and handed them back to everyone.

'So, this place is where Finlay must have been taken to. It's not very big, is it? Not for a war room anyway,' Eve said, standing up slowly.

'I don't think this *is* the war room,' said Uncle Rufus. 'It seems to me that this would once have been a guard room. I think the war room must be through that door. Come on, everyone, help me to open it.'

'Hang on a minute,' said Eve, pulling her uncle back by his arm. 'Have we forgotten that something or someone just punched you and threw you to the ground! Are we all sure that we want to carry on?

'I think that whatever it was that attacked the professor was a guardian of some sort,' said Clovis. 'It doesn't want us here. It wants us to go.'

'Oh God, I hope he doesn't try to stop us again,' whispered Tom under his breath.

'I think you might be right, Clovis,' agreed Uncle Rufus. 'Maybe it was a ghost of a German officer who stayed here, listened to the radio and —' He swept his hand around the room — 'ate here, slept here. He was a guard, a soldier, and now a ghost that still believes the war is raging and still believes his job is to protect the war rooms. That's why I'm on the right track and I think what we are looking for is on the other side of this door.'

The door was incredibly heavy, but with all of them pulling on the handle, the structure eventually began to give way. It opened slightly, dust and plaster coming away like falling snow. They heaved with all their might, paying no attention to the groaning and creaking of the hinges that had rusted over with time.

Once they had opened it wide enough for everyone to get through, Uncle Rufus dragged over the sideboard with the radio on it and wedged the door open. 'Just in case.' He winked at his niece, and then one by one they stepped through into the inky blackness.

CHAPTER 18

Silence at All Times

A pitch-black, foreboding underground passageway opened up before them. Everyone stared, not quite believing where they had come to. Boris interrupted their worried thoughts by giving one loud bark, which of course made everyone jump.

'What is it, Boris?' asked Eve. She bent down, rubbed his ears and stroked him.

'Right, everyone, stick together,' said Uncle Rufus over his shoulder.

'Don't worry, I'm not going anywhere on my own,' said Tom, shivering.

Several doorways sat on either side of the dark corridor. The doors hung open, partially covering what lay inside. Eve shuddered. The darkness stretched out before the group, black brick walls surrounding them as they moved slowly together. No clues were visible as to where they had come to or what the place was used for.

Tom looked back at the guard room door still standing open, inviting them to return. It slowly began to disappear into the darkness the further they walked away. He hoped it wouldn't be long until they were back in it, taking the elevator and trundling up to the surface.

'So do you think this definitely leads to the underground war rooms?' asked Eve. She held onto Clovis's arm and with her other hand clutched at Tom's sleeve.

'Only one way to find out,' said Uncle Rufus.

They scanned the walls with their torches, looking for some sort of writing, a clue perhaps as to where this place led to — but nothing. An inky thick blackness covered them like a fog.

Old electricity cables hung above their heads, from which dusty, blackened lightbulbs swung in the breeze that the unexpected visitors made as they walked further into the darkness.

'It's a shame they don't work,' muttered Tom, flicking a lightbulb back and forth.

'I don't think this tunnel is too long,' whispered Clovis.

'It's not how long it is but what's at the end of it that I'm more worried about,' said Eve, squeezing Clovis's arm even tighter.

Boris barked again, the noise echoing all around them.

'Look, here,' said Uncle Rufus, positioning his torch onto the right-hand side of the wall where a huge black Nazi swastika had been painted. Some of the paint had started to flake away but there it was, big and bold for all to see, the famous sign that humanity had come to fear and hate.

Clovis noticed a face looking at them from further down the corridor. He took a step back and gasped.

'What is it?' Eve asked, concerned.

Clovis walked forward from the rest of the group and slowly moved towards the shadowy face. As he got closer, he realised it wasn't a ghost at all, but a painting on the wall. Relief rushed through him. 'Look at this!' he cried.

Another portrait of Hitler stared back. Up close, Clovis felt his skin crawl. In this torchlight, Clovis could be looking straight at the real man. The picture was so lifelike. Black eyes penetrated his own, making Clovis feel very uncomfortable. Even now after all these years, there was something so evil about this creature. Everyone gathered round and stared at the monstrous image. No words were uttered, no one needed to say anything.

It was Uncle Rufus who broke the silence. 'I think we've found the war rooms,' he said, walking forward slowly in wonder.

'How do you know?' asked Tom, quickly following.

'That sign,' said Clovis, pointing to some black words that had been painted on the wall: *JEDERZEIT STILLE.*

'What does it mean?' questioned Eve, running her hand over the crumbling black paint.

'It means *silence at all times*,' said Uncle Rufus. He now stood in front of the first doorway on the left of the corridor. He moved his torch around, lighting up what was inside.

The others shuffled to join him, constantly looking about

them, their nerves on edge, not knowing what was about to come their way.

They didn't have to wait long to find out. Huddled in the doorway, they pointed their torches into a dark room. An old metal bed sat in the corner and in the middle of the room was a desk, on it an old-fashioned typewriter and a rather large black telephone.

'I imagine this room would have belonged to a secretary of some sort,' said Uncle Rufus. 'The person who worked here would have been a dogsbody to someone important.'

Just as he stopped talking a very loud knocking noise could be heard.

'Where's that coming from?' asked Eve, walking into the small room.

'I can't pin it down to one area,' said Uncle Rufus, joining his niece inside the cramped space.

'It sounds like a heartbeat. Listen,' said Tom, leaning into the wall. 'It's coming from *the walls*.'

Clovis moved quickly and placed his stethoscope up against it. Eve let out a little laugh. Clovis looked like a mad doctor as he searched the wall for the noise.

'Tom's right. The noise *is* coming from over here,' he said.

The knocking noise turned into loud thumping noises. *Thump . . . Thump . . . Thump.*

It seemed the ominous banging had moved from the walls and was now all around them. It was terrifying.

'What is it?' shouted Eve, her hands now over her ears and her face etched with fear.

Suddenly the menacing sound stopped. Everyone held their breath. No one moved a muscle for what seemed an age, waiting to see if the noise would come back.

'That was very bizarre,' whispered Clovis.

'It was bloody terrifying,' said Eve, pulling her collar further up around her neck.

'Let's keep going,' said Uncle Rufus quietly. They all began to move silently towards the door on the opposite side of the corridor when Clovis jerked around quickly, facing the doorway they had just come from.

'What is it?' asked Uncle Rufus.

'Did one of you just shush us?'

'I didn't,' said Eve.

'Neither did I,' said Tom, looking worried.

'Nor me,' said Uncle Rufus.

'Well, someone just shushed us, I definitely heard it. It was very clear.' Clovis still had the stethoscope stuck in his ears.

Just then Tom dropped his torch on the floor. It clattered and rolled about, making its light cast dancing dark shadows over the black tunnel walls. Then he pointed and whispered in a shaky voice, 'Look!'

Everyone whipped round to see a ghostly German soldier sitting at the table in the room they'd just left. He was writing furiously on something. Then he suddenly looked up, pressed his forefinger to his lips and made the shush noise again.

He was quite young-looking and dressed in a Nazi uniform of steel grey trousers and matching jacket. By the side of his desk leaned a rifle, presumably for use at a moment's notice.

The ghost was slightly transparent and his actions were slow yet fluid. Everyone watched on in astonishment, wonder and fear. The spirit carried on writing, seemingly not too bothered by the rude interruption. Then he picked up the phone and began to dial.

'Can he see us?' whispered Eve, who was completely mesmerised.

She stepped nearer to the ghost, hardly believing her eyes. She walked slowly and quietly back into the room. She had no idea why she was walking forward, she almost seemed propelled by some kind of mysterious force. The apparition was so close now, she could almost touch it. She was just about to do that, when without any warning the ghost snapped his head round, looking straight at her. Eve froze in terror. She was staring straight into the face of a ghost. His skin was transparent and his eyes were dark menacing holes. The ghost's gaze bored into her soul and Eve gasped and felt her stomach flip. She thought she might throw up. Squeezing her eyes tight shut, she willed the apparition away. A second later she slowly opened them again, hoping that it had indeed disappeared.

But no such luck. It was still very much there, and now

it was even closer, staring hard into her face. Eve felt entombed inside her own body, every fibre of her being was screaming for her to run, but something was stopping her. She couldn't even put one foot in front of the other. She realised she was frozen in fear. Could the ghost see her? Eve hoped not.

Then to everyone's horror, the spirit seemed to snap out of its dreamlike state. It stood up, then, in a weird unnatural jerky manner it walked around the table, seemingly about to make a grab for Eve.

Uncle Rufus rushed in and threw both his arms over his niece, and as he did so, the terrifying ghostly spectre vanished into thin air.

'You OK?' asked Tom, rushing forward to his friend's side.

'Yeah . . . but what the hell *was* that?' asked Eve, visibly shaking.

'That was amazing,' sighed Uncle Rufus, 'that's what it was. What a terrific experience. I just hope the cameras picked it all up.'

'Terrific for you, maybe, but I've never been so scared in my *life*. I thought he was going to hurt me.'

'You were very brave, my dear girl.'

'It seemed like he couldn't hear or see us,' said Clovis.

'I believe,' said Uncle Rufus, 'that we've just witnessed a ghost that is replaying a moment of his life. It wouldn't surprise me if we see him do the same thing again and again.'

'That's the stone tape theory, isn't it?' added Clovis,

looking very satisfied with himself. He really had done his research into the paranormal world.

'Exactly, Clovis.' Uncle Rufus grinned and patted Clovis on the back.

Eve and Tom looked at their friend and waited, knowing that a long explanation was coming.

'Keep it short,' Tom said, rolling his eyes at his friend.

As they walked out of the room, Clovis explained the theory that some scientists thought was the cause for certain hauntings.

'Ghosts of Roman soldiers have been seen marching through walls, a whole funeral procession from the Victorian era has been witnessed regularly in the driveway of an old stately home. There are many hauntings where the ghosts do not interact with the living and they seem to be doing what they did when they were alive. Scientists believe that the stones can record sound and vision in and around a building and then when the conditions are right – atmosphere, pressure, temperature – the stones act as a projector. Playing out images that we get to see.'

'I kind of get it,' said Tom. 'So, it's like memories of the past being played out?'

'Precisely,' nodded Clovis.

'Well, if I hadn't seen that ghostly soldier with my own eyes, I would think that theory was a load of old rubbish,' said Eve. 'But . . . the ghost seemed to be looking straight at me. How odd, are you sure he couldn't see me?'

'I don't think so,' said Uncle Rufus. He was sweeping his torch around the small corridor, trying to see which room to venture into next. 'I believe that soldier was an image of a memory where perhaps he was annoyed at being disturbed, and if anyone did, then God help them. Does that make sense?'

'I think so,' said Eve, clinging onto her uncle's sleeve.

'What do you think that thumping noise was, though?' asked Clovis, looking over his shoulder just to make sure the ghost had definitely disappeared. His nerves were now getting the better of him. 'It sounded like a heartbeat to me. What do *you* think it was, Professor?'

'I've witnessed that before. It's strange; that type of knocking always seems to occur just before something is about to happen, like a warning, almost. You all OK?'

They nodded as convincingly as they could. Uncle Rufus brought his torch back to his young companions and smiled at them. His smile was sweet and sincere as he delivered a statement that ripped fear into their hearts.

'I think we need to split up now,' he said, looking at his watch and avoiding their eyes. 'I don't want us to get tired, that's when mistakes can happen, and we don't want any injuries. The sooner we can get out of this place, the better. In paranormal investigations it's usually advised that a group larger than three should split up. You cover more ground that way, and hopefully in doing so, we will find Finlay a lot quicker. What do you think?'

Uncle Rufus was met with stares of surprise and bewilderment, along with a stony silence.

'Come on, it makes sense,' he said. 'Although, if you don't want to, I'll totally understand.'

Clovis was the first to speak up. 'I agree with you, Professor. I'm happy with that.'

'OK, I suppose so,' said Tom, 'as long as I'm not on my own.'

'No one will be on their own and we will still be able to hear each other. This place isn't big, so we can't go that far.'

'It does make sense, Uncle ... as long as I can go with you and Boris,' smiled Eve.

'You boys OK with being together?' Uncle Rufus asked the others, who were now looking very uncomfortable. Tom was biting his thumb again and Clovis's glasses had steamed up, a sure sign that he was very nervous. But they nodded again, despite themselves.

'OK, Eve and I will take the left-hand side of the corridor and you chaps take the right. If any of us gets into trouble, call out. Always keep each other in shouting distance.'

Everyone agreed and they split up, parting ways in the middle of the corridor. Uncle Rufus, Eve and Boris went into the next room on the left-hand side and the boys walked into the room opposite on the right.

Tom and Clovis couldn't believe their eyes. In front of them, through the gloom, they could just make out a room filled with long cabinets, hundreds of different coloured wires spewing out, entangled together like colourful spaghetti. Different coloured telephones nestled together on a desk at the back of the room.

'This would have been the communications room, I guess,' said Clovis, pulling a red wire out of its socket and pushing it back into another hole in the cabinet.

'Stop fiddling about,' warned Tom. 'Wow! So, this was like where the Germans got all their instructions. This is immense, Clovis.' Tom walked about the room, forgetting temporarily about ghosts and hauntings.

'This underground bunker must have taken them years to construct, I mean, how did they get all the equipment down here in the first place without being seen?' asked Tom.

'Yeah, I know what you mean. I don't think we'll ever know.'

They walked along the cabinets, side by side, imagining the people working here. What did they do and what secret conversations had they listened in on?

Just as they reached the end of the room, one of the telephones rang out.

Both Tom and Clovis screamed out in terror.

Tom clutched his chest, panic written all over his face. Clovis dropped to the floor in shock.

The phone continued to ring, its shrill, angry, clanging echoing about the room.

'Tom, pick it up!' shouted Clovis, standing up quickly to be close to his friend.

'Why me? *You* pick it up!'

'I've had enough of spooky telephones, you do it.' Clovis pushed Tom towards the red phone as it jingled and bounced about on the desk.

Tom leaned forward, and just as he was about to pick it up, the phone next to it began to ring as well.

'Oh my God! This is really creepy,' shouted Tom, snatching his shaking hand away.

'OK, I'll pick up the red one, you pick up the white one,' commanded Clovis, stepping forward now.

They looked at each other and counted, 'One, two, three!' Together they grabbed their individual phones, and instantly the cacophony of noise died. Tom and Clovis brought the receivers up to their ears very slowly.

Tom scrunched his eyes shut tight in readiness for a voice that would terrify him.

Clovis pushed a long breath out and looked at his friend. At exactly the same time, both boys slammed the phone down.

'What did you hear?' asked Tom, shaking all over.

Clovis was stunned and slowly looked up at him. 'I heard a man say "*Shhhh . . .*"'

CHAPTER 19

The Man in the Mask

Tom and Clovis rushed out of the communications room. They stood in the middle of the corridor and were relieved to see Eve, Uncle Rufus and Boris emerge from the darkness.

'Were you messing about with phones?' enquired Uncle Rufus. 'Eve and I heard them ringing.'

'Yeah, oh my God, Professor, the telephones rang all on their own. We couldn't believe it and when we picked them up we heard a man's voice on the other end of the line. I'm thinking it was the ghostly soldier we saw earlier. He told us to shush again. We both heard it,' said Tom, looking about him nervously.

'I just hope the watches picked up the noise,' said Clovis. 'I can't wait for us all to hear it. What about you?' Clovis was in his element. He wasn't scared any more, just excited.

'We haven't experienced anything, and there's no sign of Finlay's body so far,' said Eve. 'That room was empty.'

'You all OK to keep going?' asked Uncle Rufus. He was keen to push on. 'The place where Finlay was killed can't be far away. I'm sure there won't be too many more rooms to investigate. So, boys, you keep going on the right and we'll do the rooms on the left.'

Everyone nodded in agreement and again they split off in different directions.

Eve, Uncle Rufus and Boris walked up the narrow corridor and discovered another little side tunnel on the right-hand side. It was smaller, and without saying a word to each other they walked slowly and cautiously down it. Boris brought up the rear, snuffling and farting as he waddled along.

'I wonder where this goes?' whispered Eve.

'I don't know, but hopefully it will lead us to Finlay.'

Tom and Clovis stepped into another room. This one was long and thin and on each side of the walls were narrow bunk beds.

'There's enough beds in here for quite a lot of people. It's bizarre to think that the enemy were down here secretly.' Tom walked down one side of the room, Clovis the other. As they came to the centre, Tom stopped abruptly.

'What is it?' asked Clovis, moving his torch about.

Tom didn't answer. Shaking, he lifted his arm and pointed to the back wall. Clovis followed his friend's terrified gaze and to his horror saw a tall dark figure standing in the corner. The man, if indeed it was a man, had his back to them. And he wasn't moving at all.

'Hello,' whispered Clovis, stepping closer to the figure.

'What are you doing?' gasped Tom, pulling his friend back. 'Let's get the professor in here. I don't like the look of this.'

Ignoring his friend, Clovis stepped forward again. 'Hello, can you hear me?'

'Please, Clovis, let's go.' Tom was really scared now. As they shuffled closer towards the dark silhouette, the temperature began to drop dramatically. Still the figure did not move.

'Get an EMF meter out, Tom, I'm just thinking it could be something simple like a mannequin, you know, the kind to hang clothes on. But if the EMF goes off the closer we get, then it's very possible it could be a ghost.'

Tom took out the little machine and held it at arm's length. Sure enough the sound of static electricity bristled around them and the lights flashed in a frenzy.

'OK, can we go now?' asked Tom, stepping back. 'I think we can safely say that that dark ghoulish-looking figure is a ghost, and I don't fancy another encounter with a dead German soldier.'

Ignoring Tom, Clovis leaned forward and brought his hand up slowly to try to touch the figure. They watched in horror as Clovis's hand disappeared right through its dark shadowy body. Tom was right, it was a ghost.

Clovis had seemingly woken something within it, as the black shape twitched unexpectedly. Its head whipped round violently, to reveal a vision that would give Tom and Clovis nightmares for years to come. The tall black figure seemed to be wearing a long black coat. On top of its head sat a German soldier's cap and fixed to it a silver badge with a skull and crossbones glinted in the torchlight. They couldn't make out its face, it was too dark, but then the ghost took one large, slow purposeful step towards them and when Tom and Clovis saw the full apparition standing in front of them, both boys knew they were in trouble. All of Tom's breath rushed from his body, Clovis's knees buckled.

The tall menacing figure towered above them both, its head bent over the two boys, as if scouring their faces. Tom and Clovis looked up to see who was peering at them, but the Nazi's face was covered completely by a horrendous black rubber gas mask. Two large glass eyeholes stared back at them and deep, rasping breaths came from the rubber face. In and out, in and out: the long, gurgling, desperate sighs of a monster. The figure raised and outstretched its long arms, making a violent movement as if to grab the boys.

Two seconds was all it took: Clovis and Tom both screamed in abject terror and clambered over each other to get out of the narrow space. Tumbling about on the floor, their limbs entwined, making it almost impossible for them to get up and make their escape. Eventually, without looking back, they untangled themselves and scrambled on their hands and knees out through the door.

Terror fizzed through their bodies as they fled the area, running down the dark corridor. They stopped suddenly and stood together, neither one ashamed of the fact that they hung onto each other for dear life. Panting and out of breath, they whipped their heads about, looking to see if the hideous entity had followed them.

'Can you see it?' gasped Tom.

'No, can you?' replied Clovis.

They both stopped breathing as the sound of loud heavy footsteps echoed from behind them.

'Can you hear that?' whispered Clovis.

'Yep, I hear it.'

They clung onto each other even tighter, terrified and glued to the spot. The footsteps were getting louder and louder, until the boys were convinced that the odious ghostly creature would be upon them at any second.

Then they heard an even worse sound. It was the noise they had both witnessed earlier. A deep rasping breathing noise, the gasping and wheezing of the gas mask. In . . . and . . . out, in . . . and . . . out. The gurgling, rasping breaths were so loud now that Clovis and Tom both knew that if they dared to even peek out into the darkness they would come face to face with a horrifying vision of the most terrible kind.

'When I squeeze your hand, Tom, just run, and keep going till we find the professor.'

Clovis squeezed Tom's hand, and the two boys ran like never before.

CHAPTER 20

A Locked Door

Uncle Rufus, Eve and Boris had discovered a large room at the end of the smaller corridor. It was the plotting and map room. According to Uncle Rufus, it would have been the central hub for the Nazi operations. In the centre was a huge map of Europe, raised on a large table. Placed all over it were small moveable swastika flags.

Uncle Rufus was in his element. He took hold of a large stick that reminded Eve of an extra-long snooker rest and began to push the little flags about on the gigantic map.

'These were to show just where the Germans had invaded and these flags presumably are to show where they *hoped* to invade.'

Three clocks had been placed over the door frame, showing separate time zones around the world. Oddly they had all stopped at the same time.

Suddenly Tom and Clovis smashed into the room, nearly falling over Boris, who was lying down, enjoying a little nap.

'Shut the door, Clovis!' shouted Tom, panting to get his breath back.

Clovis slammed the door shut and leaned with his back to it, sliding down until he flopped upright onto the floor.

'What on Earth . . . Tom, Clovis are you all right?' Uncle Rufus went over to the two boys. Clearly something bad had happened to them. 'Calm down, chaps!' he whispered. 'Whatever it was has gone now. Are you both all right?'

Tom was as white as a ghost himself and Clovis was shaking.

'Never in my life have I seen something as dreadful as that,' stuttered Tom.

'Wait till you see it, Professor. It will blow your mind.' Clovis's glasses had completely steamed up. He ran his hands over his head and breathed out a nervous heavy sigh.

'I just hope the cameras caught whatever it was,' said Uncle Rufus, moving towards the door. 'Shall we go and see if it's still there?' he asked rather excitedly.

'No way!' shouted Tom. 'I never want to see that thing again.'

'What was it, exactly?' asked Eve, not quite sure if she wanted to hear the answer.

'I think what we saw was the ghost of another German soldier, but he was wearing some sort of black peaked cap with a skull and crossbones on it and a . . . a . . .' stuttered Clovis.

'Some sort of mask,' finished Tom.

'That sounds to me like he could have been an SS soldier. They were the worst, and did the most evil deeds imaginable. We need to stay clear of him,' Uncle Rufus said, scribbling in his little notebook before promptly putting it back in his pocket. 'C'mon everyone, I know it's very scary, but we have to continue. I don't believe there are many more rooms to look in. This map room certainly isn't where Finlay was brought to.' Uncle Rufus pulled on the door handle, but to his surprise the door wouldn't open. He tried to pull it again but nothing would budge.

'No, no, no!' shouted Eve, panicking. The last thing she wanted was to be locked in down here. She quickly joined her uncle and began pulling on the door handle. It wouldn't give an inch. They all tried desperately to get it to open but it was no use.

They were trapped and felt utterly helpless. What had locked them in? Was this a faulty door or the work of something paranormal?

'You don't think the ghost in that gas mask has locked the door, do you?' asked Tom, looking very worried.

'It seems nothing's impossible down here,' replied Clovis, trying again to pull the door open.

'It looks like the old trick of locking doors has come back to haunt us.' Uncle Rufus grimaced at his own awful joke, then began taking pictures of the door that had blocked their exit.

After many attempts it was clear that the door wasn't going to budge. Everyone sat on the floor and decided to take a breather.

'If we have managed to capture that horrible ghost on the

cameras, I'm telling you, I don't want to see it.' Tom shuddered at the memory of it.

Clovis put his arm around his friend's shoulder. 'It will be all right, Tom, at least we can say we've come face to face with the ghost of a gas-mask-wearing German soldier. Not many people can say that.'

Tom tried to smile.

'This room looks important,' Clovis continued, looking about in awe. He stood up and walked over to the huge map, picked up one of the little flags and began to twiddle it around with his fingers. Just as he replaced it on the table an enormous bang exploded from beneath, sending him scuttling backwards in fright.

Tom, Eve and Clovis huddled together for security. Uncle Rufus's EMF machine flashed furiously, letting them all know that they were no longer on their own.

BANG! Again, the table thumped, sending all the little flags flying through the air.

Uncle Rufus brought out the communication board and set it up on the table.

'Who is with us? Tell us your name,' he commanded sternly. The little board lit up and very quickly the knocking noises began to tap out a word.

Everyone gasped with surprise when the electronic voice said 'Finlay.'

'I was wondering when he was going to show up,' said Tom under his breath.

'Well, hello, Finlay! Can you tell us, are we close to finding you?' asked Uncle Rufus, his nose practically pressed up to the board.

The knocking continued, the board flashed away, lighting up different letters. The letters came in quick succession, then there was a pause followed by the electronic voice. It said 'Yes . . . next room.'

'Right,' said Uncle Rufus, ready to switch the board off and move. But just as he was about to, some more knocking sounds came from the floor and the table.

'Looks like he's not finished yet,' said Clovis, walking closer to the board.

Eve and Tom joined him. Gathering around the device, they all waited to see what the spirit of Finlay would spell out next.

S.T.O.N.E.

'What the hell does that mean?' asked Tom, shaking his head in confusion.

The knocking continued even quicker now. It spelled out the word *F.I.N.D.*

'Now I'm totally lost,' said Eve. 'What does he mean?'

'Well, let's go into the next room and hopefully we will find out. Let's try the door again.'

Everyone gathered round it and began to pull; it flew open so quickly that Eve and Tom ended up on the floor.

'I've a feeling that Finlay locked that door,' said Uncle Rufus, smiling. 'I think he wanted us to hear about the stone.'

'It must be very important,' said Eve, brushing herself down and following her uncle out of the map room.

'Keep your eyes peeled for this stone.' Uncle Rufus shrugged his shoulders; it was clear to the others that he too was slightly bewildered by the message that Finlay had just given them. They all made their way out of the map room and began the short walk back up the small passageway towards the main corridor. When they reached the top they stopped, took stock of where they were, and after a moment Uncle Rufus motioned for them to follow him to the right. Sure enough they came upon another door on the right-hand side of the wall and, thankfully, a dead end.

'Well, we can't go any further,' said Clovis, looking at another faded swastika on the wall. It bore down on them like a heavy black weight, reminding them just what a hideous place this once was, and what it represented.

'So, this door on the right must be the last room that we haven't checked. Let's hope Finlay is in here,' said Uncle Rufus, pushing open the final door.

One by one they walked through, taking it slowly, as there were three small concrete steps that led down into what seemed like a small cave.

'I don't like this at all,' said Eve, hanging onto her uncle.

Boris gave one loud bark and began to whine.

'It's all right, B—' Tom was interrupted by a very loud

scream. Eve was pointing at something propped up in the corner.

'Calm down, Eve, it's all right. I know it's not a nice thing to see, but remember, he's not in his body any more.'

It seemed at long last they had found Finlay.

CHAPTER 21

Finding Finlay and the Stone

In the corner of the tiny room sat the skeleton of a man dressed in dusty clothes. He was leaning against the walls; his jaw open as if still silently screaming, making his onlookers aware that his last moments had been torturous.

'Are you all right, everyone?' asked Uncle Rufus, hugging Eve close to him.

Three small voices whispered back that they were. Everyone just stood staring, not quite believing what they were seeing.

'Poor Finlay, what he must have gone through,' sniffed Eve.

'Look, Professor, can you see the hole in his skull? Is that a bullet hole?' asked Clovis, who was now leaning over the skeleton inquisitively.

'I should imagine that, yes, that is what killed him,' said Uncle Rufus, looking on sadly.

'So that's why when we first saw his ghost, he had blood running down his face,' said Eve. A single tear now ran down her cheek.

'He doesn't have any shoes on, either,' said Clovis.

'That explains the bloody footprints, too,' said Tom. 'Poor man.'

'I bet if we showed the bullet to the police — the one that was thrown at you, Eve — they might be able to match it to the damage in Finlay's skull.' Uncle Rufus was beginning to piece things together now.

'This room is terrible, it's so small,' said Clovis, bending forward and trying hard not to hit his head on the wet ceiling.

'Now we are here, what do you think Finlay wants us to do?' asked Tom, cautiously.

'Well,' said Uncle Rufus, 'just finding his body is a start, but I think there is something else he wants from us. If we go off the words he tapped out on the communication board, he said . . .'

'"Stone" and "Find",' mumbled Eve, still finding it hard to look at Finlay's skeletal remains.

Clovis began to shine his torch along the walls. Realising what he was doing, Tom joined in.

'Good thinking, Clovis, maybe there's a loose stone in here. It could be a clue for something Finlay wants us to discover,' said Uncle Rufus. He was now walking slowly around the room with Eve. They both shone their torches slowly across the black bricks that lined the bottom of the cave-like structure.

As Eve moved her foot, she stepped on something unsteady. Bending down, she located a stone that wasn't set into the floor. It was different from all the other bricks. It reminded her of a wobbly tooth.

'I think I've found something,' she said.

Everyone bent down, and with the help of Uncle Rufus's penknife, they eventually prised the loose stone out. At first glance it was very disappointing: there was nothing unusual about it. But when Clovis turned it over, there, scratched onto the hard surface, was some faint writing.

'What does it say? I can't see in this light,' said Uncle Rufus scrunching his eyes together.

'It looks like a lot of numbers,' said Tom.

'I know what they are!' cried Clovis excitedly.

'What?' whispered Eve.

'They're coordinates.'

'Coordinates?' asked Tom, looking confused. 'Coordinates for what?'

'Look here.' Clovis read out the numbers and letters slowly. They were: $51°03'41.1"N \quad 1°18'32.5"W$

'So, the line of latitude is fifty-one degrees, the oh-three is minutes and the forty-one point one is seconds, the N stands for North. The line of longitude is one degree, eighteen minutes, thirty-two point five seconds and the W stands for west.'

'Yes, that's great, Clovis, but I still don't understand what it all means,' said Eve, becoming a little impatient.

'What Clovis is trying to say is that Finlay has left us some coordinates to find something. What that "something" is, we won't know until we leave here. We have done what we came here to do. We've found Finlay.' Uncle Rufus smiled sadly.

'What do we do now, Uncle?' asked Eve.

'We go back up to the surface and I'll telephone the police. Then I suspect they'll come and recover Finlay's remains and Jane will be able to know that her father is at peace at last.' Uncle Rufus took the stone and put it into his rucksack.

Just as they began to walk out of the room, Boris barked, his little bottom wiggling with excitement.

'Uh oh, we know what that means,' said Tom, looking about nervously again.

The cold rushed in suddenly, a huge draught of iciness that took everyone's breath away. Clambering together, they waited for a ghostly presence to make itself known.

'Just when I thought we could go,' muttered Tom, rolling his eyes.

Boris seemed to agree and backed up so far that he plonked his furry bottom on top of Tom's foot and farted.

'Boris!' cried Tom.

Normally the others would have laughed, but something was happening in the room that was far more interesting.

A shadowy figure walked slowly into the cell. No one could make out what it was. A ghostly German soldier? Or the spirit of the secretary? Everyone backed up until the cold wall stopped them moving any further.

'Please don't be that ghost with the gas mask,' whispered Tom.

'I don't think it is,' said Uncle Rufus, stepping forward slightly.

The figure was closer now, and they could all make out who it was. Finlay. Standing before them in his soldier's uniform. And he wasn't angry any more. He looked at them all slowly and then suddenly a huge bright light came from above. It was so bright that everyone shielded their eyes. It flooded the tiny room, seemingly making the dirty walls and floor disappear. The atmosphere changed from a claustrophobic damp, black tomb into a space filled with love, peace and ethereal light.

'Oh my God, what's happening?' cried Eve.

'Don't worry, chaps, I've heard about this. I think we are about to witness something quite extraordinary,' said Uncle Rufus, looking like he might explode with wonder.

Indeed, something extraordinary did happen. Finlay spun around as if someone were calling him. Then he turned back and walked slowly towards Eve, Uncle Rufus, Tom and Clovis. Everyone held their breath, not quite believing what they were seeing. Tom rubbed his eyes, Clovis quickly wiped his glasses and Eve just stared, tears welling up in her eyes.

Finlay's handsome young face was just inches away from the group. It was like looking at something through clear rippling water, not quite of this Earth and yet still somehow seemingly connected by thousands of silver threads. The apparition gave the most beautiful smile and then he said faintly: 'Thank you.'

And with that, Finlay turned around and walked into the centre of the bright white light. Just as quickly as the light had arrived, it disappeared, taking Finlay with it.

The awful prison-like room that had been where poor Finlay met his death had been unexpectedly flooded with a feeling of love and joy and then just as quickly, it was plunged back into feeling like a dark, evil place once more.

Everyone stood in silence, stunned, yet overjoyed at what they had just seen.

'Did we all just witness that?' asked Clovis in a daze.

'Yes, we certainly did,' replied Uncle Rufus proudly.

'I can't believe it, I really can't,' said Tom.

'Me neither, it was just incredible, wasn't it? I mean *wow*!' said Eve. Her voice was getting louder and louder with excitement.

'Right,' said Uncle Rufus in a purposeful voice. 'We have to go back upstairs and call the police. They will need to come and sort out poor Finlay's body.' They all looked down at the skeleton. 'But before we do, I just want to check something.'

He took out the EMF device and turned it on. It was the first time that it had remained silent. No lights flickered.

'I thought as much. No activity,' he said, placing the device back into his rucksack. 'The atmosphere seems to have changed too. I wonder if Finlay's spirit leaving has pushed the other spirits away too?' Uncle Rufus seemed to be talking to himself as he made his way towards the door.

'Well, that's a relief,' said Tom. 'I don't think I could cope seeing any more ghosts right now.'

'I think Finlay has definitely gone,' said Eve, smiling.

'I wonder where to and what it's like there?' wondered Tom.

Clovis remained silent. His brain was whirring as he just stared at the wall.

His friends knew something was on his mind.

'What's up?' asked Tom.

'I'm just thinking about those coordinates and what they could mean.'

'Well, let's get back, and we can start putting everything together. The sooner we get the police down here, the better.' Uncle Rufus led the way out of the small, claustrophobic room.

The others were only too pleased to leave the cell behind and go back towards the elevator. Everyone was relieved not to have any further paranormal encounters on the way. Maybe it was true. Maybe all the ghosts had now left.

Never had the friends been so happy to see an old elevator. It sat waiting for them. The door was open just as they had left it. They all squashed in, closed the rusty old gate and pressed the button to go up. At first nothing happened, and everyone looked to each other nervously. But just like before, the lift jolted suddenly into action and slowly it began to rise.

Once at the top, they disembarked and walked out of the house without a backwards glance.

Eve breathed in the fresh air, and turned her face up to the cold drizzling rain. 'That feels so good,' she said, smiling.

'What a night,' yawned Tom.

'Absolutely fascinating,' said Clovis. 'I can't wait to go over all our footage and plug our watches into Messenger One.'

'That's something we will definitely do tomorrow, but for now,' said Uncle Rufus, unlocking the car door, 'I want you all to sit in here while I phone the police.'

Eve, Clovis and Tom were all woken up by the flashing blue lights of police cars and vans. Boris didn't move a muscle. He continued to snore softly, comfortably splayed out over Tom and Clovis's knees.

'That'll be the police, then,' said Tom wryly, closing his eyes and resuming his sleeping position on Clovis's shoulder.

'Who's the professor talking to?' asked Clovis, leaning closer towards the windscreen, much to the annoyance of a dozing Tom.

'Dunno,' replied Eve. She too was squinting her eyes to try to get a better look.

Uncle Rufus was standing on the road in front of a police car's bright headlights. He was clearly explaining to a strange-looking lady just what they had found. Then he handed over the stone, before hugging her, which seemed a very peculiar thing to do.

The woman in question was small in stature and comfortably round. They couldn't see her face, as her back was turned to them. Her attire was unusual for a police officer: a scarlet cape billowed about her in the wind, and her matching hat sat lopsided on her short grey curly hair.

Uncle Rufus walked quickly back to the car, opening the door and letting in the rain and wind. He spoke quickly, shouting over the horrible weather.

'I won't be long, I'm just taking the police below, they need to see Finlay's remains. Stay here, won't you, and don't move,' he ordered. Shutting the door, he dashed back over to the strange-looking lady, where they exchanged more words, then walked through the trees, followed closely by several police officers.

As the birds began to sing their dawn chorus, Uncle Rufus climbed back into the car. He started the engine, and in doing so, woke up its sleeping occupants again.

'Everything all right, Uncle?' asked Eve, yawning.

'Yes. It's all sorted. I can't wait to get home, can you? I think a cooked breakfast first, followed by some sleep.' Uncle Rufus began to hum a tune as he drove the car out of the forest.

'Uncle, who was that woman you were talking to? You know, the one with the cape?'

'Oh, that's Detective Inspector Rutherford. You'll be introduced soon enough. She's very keen to meet you all.' Uncle Rufus smiled at his niece, and continued to hum cheerfully as he drove the little Mini all the way back to Whitechapel.

CHAPTER 22

Analysing the Evidence

After some breakfast and much needed sleep, everyone agreed to meet up in the attic later that afternoon. Uncle Rufus was already there by the time Eve, Tom and Clovis climbed the stairs and knocked on the door. They found him moving quickly between the equipment, writing things down on a clipboard; he looked very refreshed and incredibly excited. Boris was obviously still tired from his nocturnal adventures, and lay fast asleep in the middle of the floor, snoring loudly.

'Well, I trust you all slept well and are ready to review our findings?' said Uncle Rufus, organising some chairs in front of a TV screen. 'Now, I've loaded all the footage from everyone's cameras. I've already viewed most of it and sent a copy through to the inspector. I think you'll find it makes for some very interesting viewing.'

He pressed the remote control and the screen lit up, showing four squares. In each square, film shot by everyone's separate camera appeared. The footage began showing Uncle Rufus handing over their watches near the car, and then continued to follow everyone's journey right to the end. From the discovery of the elevator, followed by their encounter with the first ghost in the guard room. Things started to heat up as they watched a replay of their spooky encounter with the German secretary. Eve, Tom and Clovis gasped in astonishment as the footage clearly showed the ghostly soldier seemingly staring straight at Eve.

'Wow!' exclaimed Tom. 'The cameras really caught it all.'

'This is fantastic, Professor,' said Clovis.

The video continued to show the rest of their adventure. The worst part was when Clovis and Tom met the gas-masked ghost. Tom held his hands over his face, as did Eve, but even though Clovis had been completely terrified at the time, he was now utterly enthralled by the images the camera had managed to capture. The horrendous supernatural vision the boys had witnessed was there for all to see. Its black gas mask loomed large on the screen. The breathing and gurgling were loud and clear.

Eve screamed out in terror: 'Oh my God, guys. I don't think I would have been as brave as you. I would have just kept running till I reached the elevator.'

'Listen, can you hear that?' asked Uncle Rufus.

Everyone shook their heads.

'All I can hear is my nightmare returning,' moaned Tom.

'I can hear words, German words, but they are definitely there.'

Uncle Rufus rewound the video and played it again.

'There, can't you hear it?' He was clearly excited now, and frustrated that the others couldn't hear it too.

'It's saying "Gefahr! Sie kommen."'

'What does that mean?' asked Tom.

Clovis stood up. He was excited now too. 'It means "Danger! They are coming."'

'Wow! So this ghost was actually warning you, not scaring you,' said Eve.

Uncle Rufus was pacing the room again. 'Yes, it's most extraordinary. The ghost can clearly see you both and he seems to believe that the war is still happening.'

'I wonder who he was trying to warn you about?' said Eve, looking confused.

'I'm thinking that maybe the Nazis knew their war rooms had been discovered and they had to make a break for it,' said Uncle Rufus.

'Yes, I think you're right, Professor. I wonder if any of them made it back to Germany?' said Clovis.

'Well, I'd never like to see that ghost ever again. Makes me go cold just thinking about it.' Tom sat back and shuddered once more.

'Well, I for one thought you were both very brave. Well done, chaps,' said Uncle Rufus, smiling. 'You kept it together, well, almost. That's very impressive.'

Then came the part where they discovered Finlay. No one said a word as they saw once more the remains of that poor man. Everyone's face was downcast but it wasn't long before the mood changed to wonder as they sat watching wide-eyed, the amazing and beautiful footage of Finlay moving towards the light. The fact that the cameras had picked up every detail was just fantastic.

When Uncle Rufus stopped the film, they all sat and talked about what they had just seen and experienced.

'Would you do it again?' asked Uncle Rufus.

'Absolutely!' cried Clovis.

'It was just the best, even though I was pretty scared all the way through,' said Tom.

'I think so,' said Eve quietly, 'but I have to admit I didn't like that ghost whispering in my ear.'

'What about the watches?' asked Clovis. 'Have you loaded the material into Messenger One yet, Professor?'

'I have,' said Uncle Rufus, 'but let's review that tomorrow. I want us to listen to the EVP material along with someone else, and they're not coming here until then.'

Everyone looked at each other, excited as to who this mystery person could be.

'Is it Jane?' asked Eve, the others nodding in agreement.

'No, but you have reminded me to do something. Let's phone her and tell her about us finding her father,' said Uncle Rufus.

He took his phone out and found Jane's number. On speaker, the phone rang only a few times before it was answered by a faint voice.

'Hello.'

'Hello, Jane, it's Rufus.'

'Oh, hello, Rufus, what a lovely surprise.'

'The kids are here with me too.'

Eve, Clovis and Tom all cheered their hellos, and then Uncle Rufus cleared his throat, took a deep breath and began to tell the delicate story of how they had discovered Finlay's remains.

After Uncle Rufus had finished, there was a long silence. Everyone looked at each other, worried that Jane had not heard or had collapsed from the news.

'Are you still there, Jane?' whispered Uncle Rufus. 'Jane!' He looked worried now, but his anguished face relaxed as he heard Jane's soft voice come through the phone's speaker.

'I can't tell you what this means to me. I can rest now, and so can my father. You have all done such a marvellous thing. I can't thank you enough.' Everyone heard Jane sniff; they could tell she was crying but also detected that she seemed to be happy in the knowledge that her father had been found at last. In the distance they could hear Mister Pig the parrot squawking away.

'Shall we come and visit you soon?' asked Eve, pushing her face closer to the phone. 'We could show you some of the footage we took.'

'Arse!' squawked Mister Pig.

'That would be lovely. I think I will be quite busy arranging a funeral, so perhaps you could come over sooner rather than later?'

'Of course,' answered Uncle Rufus. 'We can help you with the funeral arrangements if you like?'

'That would be super,' answered Jane. 'You're all too kind.'

'Big hairy bum!' squawked the parrot.

Eve, Tom and Clovis covered their mouths in a desperate attempt not to laugh out loud at the potty-mouthed bird.

'I'm sorry about Mister Pig. I think I've given him too much to eat today. When I do, he gets so naughty.' Jane was obviously embarrassed by the rude bird. 'Naughty boy, stop it at once but . . . Mummy still loves you.' Her voice cooed and ahhed at the foul-mouthed animal.

The others could just imagine the scene on the other end of the phone and began to giggle.

'How about we come over tomorrow evening?' suggested Uncle Rufus.

'Perfect, I shall have the tea and cake ready,' replied Jane.

After they had all shared their condolences and repeatedly asked if Jane would be all right on her own tonight, and once she had convinced them all that she would be, Uncle Rufus and the others said their goodbyes and rang off.

'That bird is hilarious!' shrieked Tom. 'God, I'd love to take him home with me one day. Just to see the look on my dad's face when he calls him an "arse"!'

Everyone fell about laughing and even Boris barked loudly.

'Jane was shocked about our discovery. But then she

seemed pleased that we'd found her dad, didn't she, Uncle Rufus?' said Eve when the laughter had died down.

'Yes, I have to admit, I was dreading having to tell her that we had found her father and that he'd been murdered, but I suppose she can rest now, knowing that he is at peace and can have a proper burial.' He stood. 'Right then, I don't know about you chaps but I'm starving. Shall we go and cook up a nice big supper? Then, I think a movie and an early night. I suspect we could all do with a good rest.'

CHAPTER 23

An Inspector Calls

The next morning, after the first good night's sleep everyone had had for a while, Eve, Tom and Clovis were enjoying a hearty breakfast. They were also happy in the knowledge that they didn't have to go to school. The rain battered against the window and Eve watched the sky change colour from a dirty grey to an angry black.

'I hate this weather,' she said, popping the last of her toast into her mouth.

'Yeah, me too. If the football fields get waterlogged we can't play,' sighed Tom.

'Well, I like this kind of weather. Just means I can spend more time indoors reading,' grinned Clovis.

'Well, I think we'll all be doing a lot of that. Unc has promised the school that we'll catch up with our work over the weekend,' said Eve, starting to clear her plate away.

'Oh no, do you think so?' moaned Tom.

'I know so, I heard him talking on the phone with the head last night. C'mon, it's not that bad, let's go find him and see if we can listen to the EVP recordings.'

Everyone made their way up the twisting staircase, including a panting, flatulent Boris. At the top, Eve knocked and opened the door.

They found Uncle Rufus twiddling with some wires on the floor in front of Messenger One.

'You OK, Professor?' asked Clovis, rushing over to assist.

'Yes, yes,' came a muffled response. 'I've just listened to the EVP recordings and I've edited it all together so now we can listen to it in full. It really is quite exceptional.' Uncle Rufus ran his hand through his hair, took his glasses off and wiped them clean with a handkerchief. 'I'm excited for you all to hear it. But I'm just waiting for our special guest to arrive.' He looked at his watch, popped his handkerchief back into the top pocket of his waistcoat and then began to pace back and forth.

As if on cue the doorbell rang: 'Ah ha! Perfect timing,' said Uncle Rufus, stepping over Boris, who was by now fast asleep. He left the room, and everyone strained their ears, listening to the voices below.

'I wonder who it is?' said Eve.

'Could be the police. The professor said they were coming over today,' suggested Tom.

Clovis had gone to the door and was leaning over the bannister to see if he could get a look at who was joining them. He came running back in. 'It *is* the police,' he whispered. 'You know . . . that strange old lady.'

Footsteps thumped up the stairs and Uncle Rufus could be heard chatting happily with the new visitor.

'Well, everyone,' he said, smiling broadly as he entered the room. 'Let me introduce to you Detective Inspector Rutherford.'

The police officer really was a strange sight to behold. She began to unbutton her red cape, which Uncle Rufus took from her. Once her red tasselled hat was dethroned, she patted her silver curly hair and clapped her hands together.

'Well, well,' she said in a very posh voice. 'I've been looking forward to meeting you all for a while. I've heard so much about you over the years.'

Over the years?

Clovis, Eve and Tom had all stood up and arranged themselves, without realising, in a line. The strange policewoman walked slowly past them as if she were inspecting the troops.

'You must be Tom, a footballer, I hear, and a very good one too.' Tom smiled and blushed bright red.

'You are Clovis, the logical thinker, the brains of the outfit.' Clovis grinned from ear to ear while Tom and Eve tried to not laugh. 'A cracking start, young man,' said the detective inspector.

And then she moved onto Eve. 'And this, of course, is . . . Eve. The curious one. I believe this latest adventure is down to you, isn't it?' The detective inspector winked as she looked closely at Eve.

Eve was about to respond but the woman held her hand up in a signal for her not to say a word. Eve closed her mouth like a trapdoor slamming shut.

'Well, now, first things first. I'm afraid I have some grave news.' Detective Inspector Rutherford looked uncomfortable. 'I'm sorry to say that your friend Jane Bains passed away last night.'

Everyone let out a gasp. Eve began to cry and Uncle Rufus looked distraught.

'Who found her?' whispered Uncle Rufus. He was looking at the floor, and no one could see his face.

'I did, Rufus,' replied the detective inspector. 'I went over there to tell her the news about the discovery of her father's body, and also to tell her what a hero he was. You can imagine my dismay when I found her. She was sitting in her chair in the front room. She must have died in her sleep. I know this sounds strange, but she actually had the most glorious smile on her face.' Detective Inspector Rutherford touched Uncle Rufus's arm gently. 'I'm so sorry for you all. I know you'd been friends for a long time, Rufus.'

'Poor Jane,' whispered Clovis. 'I really liked her.'

'Yeah, me too,' said Tom. 'We were going to see her this afternoon.'

'She must be with Finlay now. I think that's why she was smiling,' said Eve, looking a little brighter.

'I think you're right, my dear,' agreed Uncle Rufus. 'It's

funny, but the last thing she said to me was that she could rest now. I think perhaps she knew she was going to die.'

'Yes, Professor,' agreed Clovis, 'it's been scientifically proven that many people know when they are about to die. I think she was ready to join her dad.'

'I know she didn't have any family, Ruthers, so I would like to arrange Jane's and Finlay's funerals.' Uncle Rufus took his handkerchief out again and blew his nose.

'Of course, and if there's anything I can do to help, just let me know,' she said. 'In fact, first things first, let me go and put the kettle on, I think we all need a hot drink.' And Inspector Rutherford bustled off down the stairs.

The others sat motionless, sad but strangely content.

'Does anyone else feel guilty for feeling happy that Jane is with Finlay?' asked Eve.

'Not at all, that's quite normal,' replied Uncle Rufus.

'It's certainly been an adventure I will never forget,' said Clovis.

'Me too,' said Tom. 'Especially all the screaming you did, Eve.'

'Me, scream? Get lost! What about you, you big cry baby.' Eve leaned over and playfully punched Tom on his arm.

Detective Inspector Rutherford coughed loudly as she came back into the room. She carried a large tray of mugs, cups and biscuits. Dark brown liquid sloshed about as she jiggled the tray into position on a nearby table.

'I made tea; it was a guess. I hope it was right.'

'Thank you, Ruthers, it's perfect. Just what we all need,' smiled Uncle Rufus.

Everyone helped themselves to a hot drink and a biscuit and began to chat, but the detective inspector had other ideas. She coughed loudly, bringing the attention back to her. She sucked in air, making a strange whooshing noise. Her mouth formed a perfect circle, and then she began to swing a clacking black beaded necklace that hung about her neck. 'So, did you all enjoy your exploits the other night?' Her head was lowered but her eyes were locked on the three friends.

Not sure how to answer, no one replied. Were they in trouble for entering the house? How much could they tell a policewoman about the paranormal things they'd seen? Would she believe them?

'Come, come,' the detective inspector continued. 'You mustn't be shy. The professor and I are old friends and he's been keeping me in the loop about your adventures.' For an old lady she certainly moved around fast. Grabbing a heavy wooden chair with gusto, she brought it over, plonked it down in front of Eve, Tom and Clovis and perched her small body on the arm.

'So, shall we listen to what you've captured on Messenger One?' she said, smiling and winking at them all.

'Erm, I didn't know you knew about my uncle's inventions, Detective Inspector,' said Eve quietly, not sure what to make of this policewoman.

'Oh, please call me Ruthers. All my friends do. I met your

uncle years ago when I was investigating a case near his university. I needed some professional advice from him about a case with a paranormal element, and we've been firm friends ever since.' She looked at Uncle Rufus fondly and fiddled with the long string of black glass beads.

'What did you make of all the footage I sent you?' asked Uncle Rufus.

'Extraordinary, quite extraordinary.' She was up now, pacing about again, hands clasped firmly behind her back. She clicked her tongue, walked over to Uncle Rufus and slapped him hard on the back. 'First rate, dear boy! I can't wait to hear what auditory phenomena you have captured.'

Tom, Eve and Clovis were dumbfounded. They looked at each other in total disbelief. How come this woman knew so much about everything and how come this was the first time they had ever met her or even heard about her?

'Chaps,' said Uncle Rufus. 'Please don't be alarmed. Detective Inspector Rutherford knows all about my work. She respects it very much and is here to help. I promise to tell you everything later.'

'OK,' said Eve quietly.

'So, we're not in trouble then?' asked Tom.

'Certainly not,' replied the woman. 'On the contrary. In fact I've come here to congratulate you. Not only have you done Finlay and Jane a great service, but you've also done a great service to the country.'

'What do you mean?' asked Tom.

Detective Inspector Rutherford sat back down on the arm of the chair, perching like a rather large bird. 'The coordinates you found on the stone are for the location of a statue of a very famous king. Alfred the Great's statue, which stands in Winchester. Do you know it?'

The three shook their heads.

'It's a beautiful monument to one of our most influential leaders in history. In his hand he holds a sword which is pointing downwards towards the plinth he stands on. Well, yesterday, a special military team went to the statue and excavated under it. To their amazement they discovered some very special top secret blueprints.'

'Blueprints? Of what?' asked Clovis, clearly very excited now. His long legs began to jiggle up and down.

'Well,' continued Detective Inspector Rutherford, 'the blueprints are for a device it seems the Nazis invented during World War Two. This invention was a weapon; in fact, it was such a powerful weapon that if built, could have obliterated cities, even countries, in a matter of minutes. Fortunately, it was never constructed but someone had the idea to hide the plans – and where better than to place them than in the care of one of this country's finest kings.' The detective inspector paused to look at the shocked faces staring back at her.

'The invention is called the "sun gun",' she continued. 'A one hundred metre diameter concave mirror that reflects the sun's rays onto the Earth. Even today in the wrong hands this weapon, if made, could be globally disastrous.'

'So, it's like a huge ray gun?' asked Tom.

'Exactly,' replied the detective inspector, smiling.

'So, who hid the blueprints inside the statue?' asked Clovis.

'Finlay did. He was an exceptional man, and one of the best undercover operatives this country has ever had. We now know that the week before he discovered the Nazi war rooms and disappeared, he had been on a secret operation in Berlin. According to government sources, his mission was to steal the blueprints of the terrifying weapon the Germans were beginning to assemble. He was obviously successful, but before moving onto his next mission, not having time to securely pass them onto the British government, he placed them into the plinth of King Alfred's statue until he could retrieve them later.'

'But why *that* statue, Detective Inspector?' asked Tom.

'We are not too sure, but what we do know is that Finlay was stationed at a secret training facility in Winchester. As you can imagine,' continued the policewoman, 'his last days in that Nazi bunker must have been terrible. Not only would he have been interrogated for British war secrets, but he must have been desperate to try somehow, some way, to leave a clue as to the whereabouts of the hidden blueprints.'

'Oh, God, he must have known he was going to die in that horrible room!' said Eve, her voice choking.

'So, he scratched the coordinates onto the stone and has been waiting for someone to come to the house all these years.' Tom was astounded, as were the others.

Detective Inspector Rutherford leaned back; a satisfied look spread across her round face. 'Indeed. When the Germans captured Finlay, all hell must have broken loose. They knew they were on borrowed time. If one British soldier had uncovered their secret bunker, how long would it be before more arrived?'

'So,' continued Uncle Rufus, 'they killed Finlay and made a dash for it.'

'It's like a war movie,' said Clovis.

'So where are the blueprints now?' asked Eve.

'They are quite safe, my dear, and thanks to you all, they will never see the light of day again. But our biggest thanks has to go to Finlay. He is a true hero, not just for the many dangerous missions he completed during the war, but for keeping such a lethal weapon out of the wrong hands. A weapon which could still do untold damage today.'

'Well, I'm shocked,' said Eve, standing up. 'All we wanted to do was have a spooky night on Halloween. It's just all so incredible.' She walked over to her uncle and placed her arms around his neck. 'What an adventure. Thank you, Uncle,' she whispered.

Detective Inspector Rutherford clapped her hands in excitement. 'Now let's get back to the phenomena you've all captured.'

'Yes, let's listen to Messenger One,' said Uncle Rufus. He stood by the huge machine, and pressed a red button under one of the ginormous horns.

Instantly the sound of static emanated around the room, then suddenly to everyone's utter delight, ghostly voices could be heard, lots of them. Men and women all talking at once. The others couldn't understand what was being said as it was all in German. Uncle Rufus translated.

'These must be the voices of all the people who worked down there. They are talking on phones and discussing an invasion. How utterly fascinating. They still think the war is occurring. They still think it's nineteen-forty!'

Clovis, Eve and Tom all recognised the soldier who had shouted 'NEIN!' at them and were astounded to hear the same voice shouting and muttering other words that none of them had heard that night.

'I can't repeat what he's saying. It's too rude,' laughed Uncle Rufus.

The watches had seemingly picked up many different voices and sounds including the shushing ghost and the terrible gas-masked apparition giving Tom and Clovis a warning. Then finally they all heard Finlay thanking them.

No one could believe just how well Messenger One had managed to interpret the voices of the dead.

The static noise came back again, and everyone waited just in case there were any more voices to come through – but there were none.

Uncle Rufus pressed another button on the machine and a little USB stick popped out of a tiny compartment.

'This is for you, Ruthers. I think it will be useful if you

need to explore the case any further. You know, put it on file.'

The detective inspector took the tiny device from him, gave him a knowing smile, then put it in her pocket.

'Well, now,' she said. 'I have to say, that was all wonderful. I have never heard such clear voices from the other side. Messenger One really is everything you said it would be and more, Professor. I don't think you realise just what an important thing you have all done. Each and every one of you has achieved amazing work.' She got off the chair and began to gather her things. She swung her cape about her shoulders and fastened it at the neck, then she plopped her red tasselled hat on her head and nodded at them all.

'You look relieved, my dears, to think this ghost stuff is over. But let me tell you, it's not. This is just the beginning. There's a lot more to do and I will be seeing you all again a lot sooner than you think.'

Smiling, she turned around quickly, causing her cape to billow out in a perfect circle, stepped over a snoring Boris, and made her way downstairs.

'Oh, by the way, I nearly forgot.' The detective inspector's voice bellowed back up the staircase. 'There's something downstairs for you all. It has no manners whatsoever. Jane's friends and neighbours didn't want it, so I thought you might.' Detective Inspector Rutherford giggled like a small child, then her footsteps could be heard trotting down the long staircase. Finally, the front door gave an almighty slam.

'What does she mean?' asked Tom, looking confused.

'I have an idea,' answered Uncle Rufus, smiling.

'Let's go and see,' exclaimed Eve, pushing everyone out of the way to get to the stairs first. They all ran down to see what the detective inspector had been talking about. Boris was the last to follow and he didn't look very happy at all.

In the hallway, placed in the middle of the floor, was a cage. And in it, sitting on his perch, was a very angry, frazzled-looking parrot.

Boris was not amused. Turning his flat nose up in the air he slowly but purposefully walked past the cage and promptly let out an enormous, raucous fart.

Mister Pig responded with some choice words that Uncle Rufus spluttered and coughed over while Tom, Clovis and Eve collapsed on the floor laughing.

'Welcome to the family, Mister Pig,' said Eve, wiping away a tear of laughter.

Mister Pig replied with one simple word.

'Arse!'

ACKNOWLEDGEMENTS

I would like to thank my husband Karl Beattie for his continued support and love. Thank you for always being there. I love you. Thank you to my wonderful children, Will and Mary. Always in my heart.

Also, Charlie Sheppard, Publishing Director at Andersen Press. Thank you for believing in me.

Chloe Sackur, Commissioning Editor at Andersen Press for making me look at things differently.

And lastly thank you, Mum. Love you.

Yvette Fielding was the youngest ever *Blue Peter* presenter at age eighteen, and she's since gone on to host and produce *Ghosthunting With . . .* and *Most Haunted*. After years of studying ghosts, she's become television's 'first lady' of the paranormal. She lives with her husband and two children in Cheshire.

Yvette's experiences of the paranormal:

In this book I have drawn upon some of my own experiences when dealing with the paranormal. I kept remembering what it was like when I ventured into my first ever haunted house. It was Michelham Priory in East Sussex. I'll never forget the fear, terror and utter adrenalin-fuelled excitement. I spent the night shaking, and doing a lot of screaming, but once it was all over and dawn arrived I just couldn't wait to do it all over again. I had been bitten by the ghost-hunter bug.

I'm fascinated by poltergeist activity. It always excites me whenever I manage to capture some movement or a flying object on camera. The bullet that hits Eve really happened to me whilst investigating RAF Raynham in Norfolk. Something hit me hard in the back, then seconds later an unseen object whizzed past my head. Everyone I was with heard these objects clatter to the floor and eventually after looking for a while we discovered two rifle shells dating back to World War Two. I have had all manner of things thrown my way, sometimes when asked for; others when not. The worst I think was a very large crowbar that missed my skull by a couple of centimetres, any closer and it could have killed me.

The knocking phenomena started happening six years into making *Most Haunted*. We were conducting a seance, another favourite experiment I like to do, when all of a sudden the *tap tap tap* sound could be felt from under the table, then it got louder and proceeded to travel about the room. At times the noise sounded like it was coming from the walls, then the ceiling and back again to the floor. When I spoke out and asked questions the knocks responded.

Over the years I have developed a way of talking to the spirits using a tapping board and to this day I'm overwhelmed with the words and sentences that are given to me from people that reside on another plane.

I have been lucky enough to see and hear ghosts, some very clearly others only partially. The first apparition I ever saw was a pair of legs walking up the main staircase in the Theatre Royal Drury Lane. They walked as if in slow motion, the image not quite solid. As you can imagine I freaked out and fled. Oh, how I wish I'd managed to stick around and film it.

My own house is haunted and when my family and I first moved in we had so much ghostly activity occur. The scariest was when I came downstairs into the kitchen to discover all the kitchen chairs were stacked perfectly in a pyramid shape on top of the kitchen table. I was dumbfounded. Why had the ghosts done this? What were they trying to say? I decided to make contact using the tapping board and discovered that the spirits of two children called Benjamin and Elizabeth, who had died in the house during the eighteenth century, wanted to play with us. We talked and told them that it was fine for them to move furniture and play games, but not to do it in the middle of the night as it was upsetting my two young children at the time. They agreed, and to this date, seventeen years later, they only come out to play when asked and believe me they have done some amazing things.

I have been investigating the paranormal since 2001 and had an incredible journey. I've witnessed full-bodied apparitions and heard their voices, been hit by numerous flying objects, and helped trapped souls reach their new home.